SEE NO EVIL

(The Gideon Kane Files)

SCOTT DELBEATO

PAGE PUBLISHING, INC.
New York, NY

First originally published by Page Publishing, Inc. 2016

ISBN 978-1-68348-158-4 (pbk)
ISBN 978-1-68348-159-1 (digital)

Printed in the United States of America

I

After a moment, Mathias felt the sting in his hand as the blood seeped down toward his fingers. As he dropped his gaze, he unclenched his fist to reveal the four tiny incisions in his palm. He rolled his hand over and stared at the crimson tinge on the tips of his fingernails as the corners of his thin, pale lips curled upward in an insidious smile.

He stood motionless behind a dark and menacing oak by the small makeshift bridge near the entrance to the park. The tired sun ebbed closer toward the horizon as the shadows awoke and took their places, concealing the hunters from the hunted. He watched as she got out of the cobalt blue Z4 coupe in the parking lot. He liked to watch them for a little while at first. He moved silently along the wood line, following her, the heavily overgrown moss dampening his footfalls. He was all but certain that the hermit thrush and the yellow-throated vireo singing in the trees by the ravine would bring her closer to him.

They love to come here and watch the birdies, the voice taunted him.

She would not be the first to disappear from this baited field. He had hunted here many times before. Women of all ages, shapes, and sizes had wandered off alone into the acres of dense and desolate woods trying to escape from the everyday bustle of the city to reacquaint themselves with the peace and tranquility of nature. It was easier for him now. Most of them walked or jogged blindly down the myriad of unmarked trails with their iPods blaring, oblivious to his presence. He took comfort in looking into their eyes as they left this world. The life did not drain from the eyes, but rather, the essence of a waning life passed through them, and he could almost see everything they had seen before the light slowly extinguished for good. Mathias had helped them all escape.

She locked her car and walked a few feet before realizing she had forgotten her prized binoculars.

Can't watch 'em if I can't see 'em, she thought.

She quickly walked back and opened what BMW had passed off as a trunk and brushed aside the papers, textbooks, and fast-food remnants that covered the interior.

"I know they're here somewhere."

She leaned far into the trunk, her small frame almost disappearing inside as she reached toward the back.

It would be easy, he thought.

Just take her right here, the voice insisted.

A little rap to the back of the head—besides, she's already in the trunk. Ah, but where would be the fun in that? Mathias liked to watch. Besides, he had gone through a lot of effort to get her here—to this very spot at this very time.

Lindsay Diaz was an attractive slender twenty-one-year-old winding down her college career at Florida State University. She had originally declared as a business major, as almost everyone does for one reason or another, before running smack dab into one too many statistics classes and finally opting for communications. Her petite frame, jet-black hair, and sapphire blue eyes would do her no disservice in the television industry. She had perfect teeth, could speak in complete sentences, and knew a thing or two about using her looks to get what she wanted. She even had some experience in front of the camera, although at the present time, only her boyfriend and his closet-hiding roommate had any idea of her true photogenic qualities.

"There you are!" she chirped, pulling the Zeiss binoculars from under an "obviously-rancid-to-everyone-else" Tropical Smoothie bag.

The Zeiss Victory series were the first to use the unique fluorite glass for superachromatic performance, she remembered the man behind the counter telling her. She didn't have a clue what "superachromatic" meant, but he said it was *the* choice for a real birder—especially a birder with Daddy's American Express Platinum card. Lindsay just knew that for two grand, she better be able to get up close and personal with some fucking birds!

She eased back out of the trunk, grabbing her recorder at the last moment before closing the lid. There was still a chance that *he* would show up, and the bird-watching story could wait. He had told her that he would meet her there at eight. She peered around the empty parking lot, and then down at her watch. She was a few minutes late. As many times as he'd tried to contact her, surely he wouldn't have left already. She would simply kill a few minutes by checking out some of the birds. He was bound to show eventually.

As she ambled toward the wood line, her Zeiss hanging from her neck like a trophy, the yellow-throated vireo caught her attention from down near the ravine. He knew it would. *He liked to watch.* She didn't know a yellow-throated vireo from a duck, *but goddamit, for two grand, she was gonna know one today! Happy, happy, happy!*

The last remnants of the day's light were easing toward the horizon, and the fleeting sunset was making it hard to see through the trees. She knew the sound was coming from near the ravine, and to the ravine she walked. The leaves and underbrush crackled under her feet, and the bird stopped singing. She raised the binoculars up to her eyes and aimed in the general direction of the ravine.

She mumbled, "Where are you, you little bastard?"

As if on cue, the vireo broke into song from the third branch of a large oak growing out of the north side of the ravine.

"There you are," she said triumphantly. She dropped the binoculars, letting them hang from her neck as she excitedly flipped through her also newly purchased copy of *Florida Bird Watching*.

"Yellow-throated vireo," she said almost disappointedly. "Looks like a canary."

She raised the Zeiss to her eyes again in the direction of the large oak and, this time, saw only darkness.

"What the hell?"

Lowering the binoculars, she spied a large balding man dressed all in black standing but a few feet in front of her. He said nothing as the corners of his smallish mouth turned upward into what she could only cerebrally process as an impish grin.

"Shit! You scared me," she said breathlessly. "Is it you? I thought I'd missed you."

He stared silently back at her as she felt the anxiousness wash over her.

She said nervously, "Hey, maybe we could go somewhere else to talk about your story. It's getting kind of dark, don't you think?"

"I like to watch too," he whispered.

She felt the sickly sweet and slightly metallic taste in her mouth as the blood trickled down the back of her throat, one of her formerly perfect teeth slicing through her lower lip.

He had closed her in seconds, and the fist struck her cleanly and squarely in both the nose and mouth. As her head struck the ground, the strap around her neck slung the Zeiss around behind her, landing between the forest floor and her shoulders. She thought she'd heard the unsettling snap as the Zeiss dug into her spine, although clarity was not abundant at this particular moment. What she did know, was that she couldn't move, and she couldn't scream. She tried. She felt the scream form in her head, but nothing happened. The only sound was the muted song of the vireo and the water trickling down below in the ravine.

As she lay there looking upward, she watched helplessly as he approached, dropping to his knees, straddling her at the waist. He leaned down over her, and she could feel his warm breath on her face as he reached down and gently held her eyes open. A fear like she had never experienced before enveloped her, and yet, all she could think of was the project she had due in Ms. Slater's video composition class on Friday. He said nothing as he glared at her, his eyes wide open as if looking for something within her—the cold empty blackness of his eyes piercing straight through her.

She has the eyes of her father, the voice whispered.

"Yes," Mathias replied softly. "Perhaps now he shall see what he has done."

Fucking birds! she thought. In this moment, all she could think to do was blame the birds. This was not how it was supposed to end.

Then, as the light began to fade and blur became pitch—she heard him.

"I like to watch."

2

Detective Sergeant Gideon Kane lay dreaming—an unimpressive one-room studio with way too high of a price tag. A few years back, the city of Tallahassee had decided that it would be a great idea to bring some life back into the downtown area by converting the old empty office buildings into precocious yuppie condos. Although the price was outrageous, the view was great, and it kept him centrally located. Save the tiny old Davenport desk which currently served as a pedestal for the twenty-five-inch HDTV, a last generation Sony boom box lying on the floor, and an obnoxious green faux leather couch that was way past its prime, there was no other furniture to be seen. The fact of the matter was that if the president of the condo association ever stopped by, she'd have thought that squatters had moved in. His mother had left him the desk when she passed away. The Davenport had originally been designed as a space-saving option to be used aboard ships in the late eighteenth century, and his mother would go on and on about how his great-great-great-uncle or some other unverifiable relative had once been a magnificent sea captain in the British Royal Navy, or something to that effect. He didn't put too much credence into her tales of the importance of their lineage considering that they weren't British, and that he got seasick watching old reruns of *Baywatch*.

The couch, which at the present time doubled as a bed, was the only piece of furniture he had kept from his college days in Tallahassee. One of the few things he'd won in the divorce. There were a lot of great memories on that couch—and under it. Not to mention the Keating twins from Delta Gamma. *Ahh, the Keating twins.*

Nights like this were rare. More than two hours of sleep at a time just didn't happen anymore. Of course, this particular slumber was facilitated by one too many gin and tonics and a six-pack of whatever beer was on sale for a chaser. How you got to sleep didn't matter anymore. If it required a little twenty-first-century pharmacology, well then so be it. Despite the old adage, the journey was highly overrated. It was the destination that mattered.

When Elizabeth had left him a year ago, he knew he couldn't stop her. It hadn't stopped him from trying though. They had just grown apart. It was better this way. That's what he kept telling himself anyway. Too many late-night cases that had consumed him and destroyed his marriage to the one woman he had ever really cared about more than himself. The only person he had ever actually opened up to and trusted. Too many corpses, too many shitheads let loose on an unsuspecting public because of an overloaded and sometimes incompetent judicial system that was set up to protect *them* instead of us. Oh yeah—and only one Gideon Kane. That was a lot of pressure for one man. Of course there was the familiarity that comes with being with someone for so long that you begin to take them for granted. *Yeah well . . . there's that,* she would say. To know that you've been tasked with single-handedly ridding the world of evil begins to wear on you a bit.

If Gideon didn't catch 'em, then they weren't gonna get caught! That's what they used to say, and Kane began to believe it.

Sixteen years as a cop, eleven as a detective, and nine with the Violent Crimes Unit can take its toll on a man. It also took a toll on his family. He'd quit once for her. For two years, he muddled through an empty existence of nine-to-five biweekly paychecks. The banking world never seemed a likely place to wind up for Gideon Kane, but he'd always been good with numbers. Kissing people's ass for the good of the company—well, that was another matter entirely. When Elizabeth's father pulled a few strings to get him a job in the investment division, he thought he'd finally be able to put all the blood and late-night phone calls behind him and live out that whole white picket fence thing. He'd breezed through all the ridiculous tests and weekend seminars that were supposed to prove that you knew what you were doing with other people's money. Who exactly decided that this qualified you as an expert was something Kane pondered every time someone asked him what they should invest in. They never listened. *Why did they ask then?* They would stare blankly and nod while he gave his prescripted presentation for forty minutes, at which time they would launch promptly into an incoherent dissertation about how Maria Bartiromo on CNBC had told them they should put all their money into online poker tournaments and some new drug that was supposed to give you the most amazing erection that modern civilization had ever seen.

Gideon lay his head in his hands listening to the extremely elderly Mr. Iozza and snore through ten minutes of this drivel before finally giving up.

God, what I wouldn't do for a corpse and some crime scene tape, he thought.

"Well"—Gideon laughed looking over at Mr. Iozza—"I guess one outta two ain't bad."

The only slightly more coherent Mrs. Iozza stared at him with a look as if he had just told her a knock-knock joke in Latin. She didn't get the irony. It was just as well.

Elizabeth sat in her office going over various writs, subpoenas, and other assorted bullshit legal paperwork that Lady Justice had decided to clog the system with. She was a divorce attorney by trade, but she did some criminal defense on the side. That's how Kane had met her. It was supposed to be simple, just a quick meeting with the state attorney to go over a case he was working. As he walked into the office, there she was. Kane was ten minutes late, but State Attorney Tom Clower motioned him in.

"I'm sorry I'm late, and I don't mean to interrupt," Kane said.

"It's all right, Gideon, we're just chatting. Do you know Ms. Pierce?"

"Elizabeth," she said, extending her hand.

Kane stood there for several moments before realizing he hadn't moved.

"Good to meet you," said Kane, finally shaking her hand with what he was sure was the clammiest handshake he had ever delivered.

That was it. That was the moment that Gideon Kane *knew*. They had begun dating almost immediately, and it just kept getting better. The conversation kept getting better. The sex kept getting better. Every time he looked into her eyes—kept getting better.

Elizabeth looked at the clock as her husband walked deliberately through her office door staring at the ground and plopping down on the blue, oversized love seat she had on the rear wall. She said it made the clients feel more at home than sitting in a stuffy, old, uncomfortable office chair. Not to mention that when you've got feuding spouses in your office, comfort is highly underappreciated, and you don't have furniture light enough to pick up and throw.

"It's two in the afternoon, why aren't you at the bank? Are you okay?" she asked, almost not wanting to hear the answer.

Kane paused for a moment.

"Apparently it is against bank policy to tell a ninety-two-year-old man with four hundred thousand dollars in your father's bank, that it doesn't matter what the fuck he does with his money because he's never gonna live long enough to spend it all."

"Mr. Iozza again, huh?" she said.

"I tried, Liz. I really, really tried . . . can I please go back to being a cop again?"

She knew better than to try and talk him out of it. It was the only thing he'd ever loved. He could do it in his sleep. He'd tried the whole suit and tie thing for her. For the sake of their marriage, maybe she could try to be a little more understanding of who her husband was supposed to be. What he was meant to do. All those nights that she'd pretended to be asleep while he got dressed when the phone rang at 2:30; all the awful things that he'd seen and never told her about. The extent to which a human being can extend cruelty to another never ceased to amaze him, and he just didn't want her to have the same dreams that he reran on a nightly basis.

It had driven him inward to the point where they didn't talk about much of anything anymore, let alone his work. She just wanted to be included in his life. He knew that. She wanted to feel as if she was as important as those families who looked to Gideon for closure. He knew that too. She had convinced him to quit the one thing that gave him purpose because she was jealous. She should have given him purpose, not those nameless faces in the dark of night.

Why wasn't she enough for him? she thought to herself. She looked up and saw Gideon staring past her, his eyes glassy.

"Because no one else can help them," he whispered.

"Guess we're moving back to Tallahassee," she said, a sarcastic grin washing over her.

The tranquility of the dark studio was shattered by the shrill of the telephone. The only other thing Kane had taken away from the divorce. Gideon barely stirred, reaching for the receiver. It was two-thirty in the morning.

"Detective Kane . . ."

"Gideon? You sound like shit."

"Thanks, Eddie. What can I do for you this lovely morning?"

"We've got a good one Gideon. Never seen one like this."

"Where?"

"We're out off of Centerville Road, near the end of Charleston, at the back of A. J. Henry Park. One of the poor schmucks on patrol pulled back here in the dark to take a leak and almost drove right over her. Well, I say *her*, at least I think it's a her."

"All right, Eddie, if it's that good, get crime scene out there and wake up the appropriate people. Is the city PD there yet?"

"Already come and gone. They took one look and said if we want it, we can have it."

"Really? Not like them to hand over a whodunnit."

"I think they're probably just cutting their losses on this one, Gideon."

"Oh, and Eddie . . . he didn't take a leak on her, did he?"

"Nah, poor rookie's ass is so tight right now he won't be able to do anything for a while."

"Do we know who she is?"

"Not yet. No ID and . . . uh, no eyes."

"Eddie, when *was* the last time we had a decent witness on a murder case?"

"No, you don't understand Gideon, there's no eyes! They're gone!"

"Gone? Animals maybe, she is in the woods."

"Not likely. This is neat, like they were scooped out or something."

"Jesus Christ, Eddie, what the fuck is going on?"

"Listen, Gideon, just get your ass down here so I don't have to be in charge out here anymore. I just want to go home and kiss my wife and daughter at this point. This is some seriously fucked up shit, man."

Raymond Edward Westin, affectionately known at the station as Eddie, was a good cop—a *very* good cop, and it wasn't like him to get rattled. Gideon sensed that there was more that Eddie wasn't talking about over the phone.

He and Gideon had started at the sheriff's office right about the same time sixteen years ago. They had both been promoted to detective within six months of each other, and a couple of years later, they had made sergeant one after the other. They had been partners while working the Burglary Division and had both been equally pissed off that they hadn't been assigned to the Persons Crimes Unit, which included Robbery and Homicide, but that's where they learned their magic. You see, what most folks outside of law enforcement don't understand is that with the exception of robbery and homicide, most persons' crimes detectives are working an inordinate number of minor assaults, batteries, and domestic violence cases. Nine times out of ten, those cases come with suspects attached. Those kinds of crimes usually take some intimacy and familiarity between a suspect and their victim. People don't normally beat the shit out of people they don't know. Therefore, there's not a lot of 'detecting' involved. It's more a matter of making sure the paperwork is in order so you don't screw the case up in court.

Burglary, on the other hand, rarely ever has a clear direction to the bad guy because most of the time, the victims, whether knowingly or not, have handed over their valuables on a silver platter. *Sure I have an alarm system officer, but I forgot to turn it on because I was in a hurry.* Burglary takes some smarts, some ingenuity, and a whole lot of creativity on the fly. Eddie and Gideon had honed their skills there, and when they both had finally made it to Homicide—they realized they still didn't know shit.

People who murder people are seriously fucking nuts, Kane thought.
Into the phone, "I'll be there in ten, Eddie."

3

Kane clicked off the phone and laid it on the floor.

"What the hell is going on in this town?" he said aloud. Gideon ran his fingers through his shortly cut salt-and-pepper hair trying to stir himself to some level of consciousness. He once had a respectable jet-black mane, cut short for comfort because summers in this town were unbearably humid and hot. That jet-black had now given way to ever-growing streaks of firmly entrenched gray. Not salt, but gray. He'd caught hell from the guys for apparently going gray overnight. Of course he blamed it on the stress of the job and Elizabeth—well mostly Elizabeth. Despite the cursory binge drinking, he kept his fairly well-sculpted, forty-two-year-old frame in pretty good shape. He had played football for the Seminoles back in the day, albeit as a kicker. Nobody appreciates the kicker, he often thought. It seemed suddenly that nothing had changed.

The screaming eagle broke his thought as the familiar refrain of the Colbert Report bellowed from the television. In a town that was so left of middle-of-the-road, Kane trusted nothing he heard on the local news, and even less of what he read in the local fish wrap. Hell, the local paper was named *The Democrat* for God's sake. *Liberals were any decent cops' bane,* he thought. Stephen Colbert was his sole source for unbiased, unequivocal truth in reporting. Not to mention a humorous respite from one too many dead bodies, grief-stricken families, and tight-assed supervisors that cared more about toeing the company line than solving cases. Still, those same supervisors knew that he was good at what he did, and they left him alone for the most part.

Gideon exited the condo, the night air hung thick around him, making it hard to breath. You just had to love summers in Tallahassee. Why people had actually settled here still remained a mystery to him. The weather was temperamental. It either rained nonstop and was unbearably hot and humid, or it didn't rain for months, and it was just plain unbearably hot.

Ahh, the luxurious Chevy Impala, he thought as he climbed into his municipally issued chariot. *Nothing sexier than a late '90s domestic,* he thought. Kane screeched out of the parking garage as he exited Kleman Plaza, left on Bronough Street, then right on Pensacola to Monroe Street. Gideon liked driving in the city this time of night. The street lamps seemed to cast an easy glow over everything, making the city seemed more at peace with itself. Sixth Avenue to Centerville Road, past the hospital and the morgue. Way too many mornings at the morgue flashed through his mind.

Why were autopsies always so fucking early in the morning? Gideon rarely felt good in the morning. Hangovers and only a couple hours sleep tend to do that to you.

The flashing red and blue strobes blinded him as he pulled to the shoulder of an otherwise dark, unassuming stretch of road on the south side of Henry Park. Eddie stood leaning back against a patrol car huffing on a Winston and shaking his head. Behind him, he spied a white lumpy sheet in the brush, the lights flickering off every bend and fold.

Eddie was skinny. Not crack skinny or AIDS skinny, but one of those types that made you sort of resent the guy as you moved into your late thirties and your metabolism took on the qualities of your ex-wife (not wanting anything to do with you anymore)—the type of guy that could run a mile with a cigarette hanging from his lips and still beat you.

Gideon sighed. "Hey, Eddie," he said, his eyes still fixated on the white cotton heap lying beyond in the grass.

"Glad you could grace us with your presence, Kane," Eddie snapped in the most sarcastic of tones.

"Whaddya got?"

"White female, maybe twenty-two . . . twenty-three. Probably used to be hot."

"Injuries?" Gideon asked, posing the obvious with a sarcasm of his own.

"T-shirt's pulled up around her neck, blunt force trauma to the face, probably a fist since I'm not seeing any pattern bruising or indentations. The mouth was stitched shut with some sort of twine or something, and she's got some kind of symbol carved in her torso. Kinda like an X over a Y."

Gideon rubbed his eyes and shook off a chill that had suddenly run up his back.

"And the eyes, Eddie?" Gideon pressed.

"Yeah, well there's that. They're gone. I went to check petechials, and when I rolled the lids back . . . they weren't there. Not to mention that the sockets are pretty clean so it's not like they were gouged out with a spoon or something."

Gideon interrupted, "Some skill . . . ?"

Eddie continued, the Winston burnt to the filter still hanging from his lip, "Yeah, there's very little trauma to the eyes and very little blood at all, Gideon. And she hasn't been here all that long, maybe a couple of hours."

Gideon wondered why Eddie would have thought to check for petechial hemorrhaging in the eyes when that would normally indicate some type of asphyxiation death. *Surely that wouldn't have been his first guess,* he thought. Gideon was meticulous that way. The fact that he couldn't grasp the logic, couldn't see where Eddie was going with that line of thought, stuck in his craw, even though, at the moment, he wasn't exactly sure where his *craw* was. When he couldn't stand it any longer, Gideon posed the question and braced for the incoming tirade he was sure was forthcoming.

"Because," Eddie snapped, "there's almost *no* blood to speak of, and her injuries, while I will admit, are just a tad fucked up, they shouldn't have been enough to kill her! And again . . . and I'm just guessing here . . . the eyes are postmortem because they're just too fucking neat, and one does not just lie still and let someone remove their fucking eyeballs without putting up a fucking fight!"

Not nearly as many "fucks" as Gideon had expected, but his point was made. Gideon sensed the obvious. He had pissed Eddie off. Veteran cops did not usually take kindly to instruction, let alone having their methods or motives questioned by anyone—let alone other cops. Although the question *had* bothered him, Gideon was only half-serious. He and Eddie had been busting each other's balls for years. That was all it was, Gideon thought, just another sack-stomping session—a good-natured kick to the cods, with maybe a little smidgeon of "Why didn't I fuckin' think of that?" sprinkled in for good measure.

Ah, well there was that . . .

"Are you finished?" Gideon quipped.

"No . . . I think she's a dump. If she was killed here, there'd be some blood, some flattened grass, broken branches . . . but there's nothin'. This is as pristine a goddamn crime scene as I've ever come across."

"So she was placed here for us to find," said Gideon.

"More like posed . . . or our bad guy was interrupted," said Eddie, pulling back the white sheet.

Gideon looked down upon the girl and saw that her arms were placed out to her sides slightly above her head, her left foot neatly draped over her right.

A crucifix? he thought.

Gideon nabbed a pair of the requisite blue rubber gloves from the bag of a none-too-attentive paramedic, and made was his way back over to the white cotton lump in the grass. The pristine white, now seemed to be speckled with little patches of black. The strobing lights of the patrol car always gave an eerie kind of blackness to the blood, and Gideon wasn't sure if what he was seeing was real, or if he was having a Lady Macbeth moment.

Out damn spot !!

Gideon knelt down beside her. The now ashen face of a once beautiful young woman—someone's sister, someone's daughter, someone's Elizabeth, someone whose tortured face would join the rank and file of the myriad of characters that would visit him at night on those rare occasions of slumber.

"Eddie, let's get her prints rolled and get 'em into AFIS before she goes to the medical examiner. Maybe we'll get lucky on the ID."

"Done, Gideon."

The automated fingerprint identification system, or AFIS, was a computer database that, theoretically at least, is purported to contain the fingerprints of anyone who'd ever been arrested for a felony crime in this country. If they were lucky, Gideon surmised, maybe this little girl had been bad at least once in her life, and they would finally know who she was, besides, he couldn't very well plaster her face all over the six o'clock news the way it was, hoping for an ID.

The vibration startled Gideon, and he fumbled for the cell phone in his pocket. The office's main number glowed on the display.

"Kane . . ." he said sternly, trying to sound official.

The sheriff's dispatcher responded in kind, "Sergeant Kane, the ME's office just called back. Dr. Jernigan says to tell you that the autopsy is set for eight this morning."

"Fabulous," Kane replied. "A mere four hours from now."

"Oh, and Kane . . . she said that if you're late this time, she's starting without you."

Why were fucking autopsies always so goddamn early in the morning?

4

A dim amber light stretched through the open doorway leading from the single bulb over the rear steps of the house onto the makeshift workbench just inside the old wooden shed. He fumbled for the switch under the shelf and heard the hum as the fluorescent bulb flickered to life, and he looked briefly away. He squinted as his eyes adjusted to the brightness looking back toward the shelf above the bench. The light caused him pain, but the fluorescents seemed to be more bearable. Neat, orderly rows of Ball mason jars lined the shelf, and he could barely make out the ambiguous annular shapes within each of them—some larger than others, some reflecting the pallid mixture of light from both the workbench and the house, the different shades of gray differentiating the blues from the greens and from the whites. He didn't need the light to see them in all their clarity and true beauty.

He reached for the second to the last jar from the right and brought it down to the bench in front of him. Twisting open the cap, he closed his eyes and removed the sole, delicate orb from its container, rolling it gently in his hands and in and out between each of his fingers. It had been his first, and one of a pair that would forever remain in his memory. The location of its mate was still a mystery. He had gone for a walk late one evening, "people-watching" at Lake Ella, and had carried them loosely in his right pants pocket, his hand caressing them as he strode around the circular path surrounding the lake, the passersby oblivious to his subdued self-gratification. The police department was right next door, at the top of a small hill to the south, and he even stopped to watch the men and women in blue change shifts mere yards away as he fondled the precious aggies right under their noses. He liked to watch.

He'd not seen it again after that evening. Perhaps it had fallen out as he quickly removed his hand from his pocket when he had noticed that one of the boys in blue appeared to be watching him.

He can't know, he remembered thinking. If he did, he would be down here in a second.

"Sir, you can't be doing that down here." The voice came from behind him, and he spun around to see a young man on a mountain bike, the single word "POLICE" emblazoned in silver across his black shirt. The officer looked down toward his pocket, his hand still firmly entrenched. He remembered feeling slightly aroused and felt something stir near his hand.

"I'm sorry, officer," he said. "It isn't what it appears. I was simply fishing for my keys."

"I'm still gonna ask that you take it to the house, sir. Hey, have I seen you before somewhere?" asked the cop.

"I don't believe so, but you're quite right. It's time I should be going."

He remembered turning quickly and walking away at what he quickly surmised was a "non-guilty pace," made it to his car, and left the parking lot, taking care to fasten his seat belt, use his turn signal, and anything else he could think of that would depict a completely innocent citizen. He was a half mile down North Monroe Street before he realized that one of them was missing, and as he had narrowly escaped the lake even though he was *sure* that they knew, there was no way in hell he was going back to look for it now.

He replaced the orb and returned the mason jar to its position on the shelf, making sure that the word "Ball" faced front, as did all the others. Even a bit askew would bother him.

"All things have their place, and all things in their place," his mother would always say. She was affectionate, overly at times, and it would not be until his early teens before he was able to discern the difference between "overly" and "inappropriately." He remembered as a child that she would insist upon things being done a certain way—her way, and he had even, on occasion, caught her spying on him making sure he was doing what he was supposed to be doing and not carrying on with the so-called *undesirables,* as she commonly referred to girls his own age.

The only woman you need to concern yourself with is the one who loves you for who you really are deep down inside, she would say as she unbuckled his trousers. He had to admit that, even for him, the first time had been kind of outputting, almost creepy, but she was his mother, and she was just trying to teach him to grow into a man, albeit for only a couple of minutes.

He recalled the first time he had been with a girl his age nearly twenty-five years ago. He was eighteen, and his mother had gone to a neighbor to play bridge on a Saturday night, and he had snuck Debbie Finch into the house. Debbie was seventeen and working on her second senior year at the high school. He had planned it well, he thought, and Debbie had been waiting outside in the backyard for him, entering the moment Mother exited the front. No time to waste. Debbie had made her way through most of the varsity teams and even a couple of the JV squads by that point, and she was not one for romance or foreplay. Right there in the kitchen, as the back door clicked shut and his mother's perfume still lingered in the air, Debbie sank to her knees and unbuckled his trousers. His eyes closed, and his legs became weak as he leaned against the back door and allowed Debbie to indulge her one talent. As he neared the point of no return and briefly wrestled with the dilemma of whether to tell her or not, he opened his eyes. There, through the kitchen and down the short hall, he spied his mother through the oval glass in the front door. She stared back at him expressionless, her eyes black and cold. She said nothing, and as he exploded into Debbie Finch, he realized—*she likes to watch too.*

5

Beep . . . Beep . . . Beep . . .

Gideon swatted blindly at the alarm and managed to catch the snooze button. He had made it back home from the park by four-thirty and had managed to fall asleep after only one Michelob Ultra and twenty minutes of lying on the couch counting the popcorn on the ceiling. Squinting through eyes caked with sleep, he picked the clock up off the floor and stared at three rather large red digital numbers that would set the tone for the day: *7:50* .

"Shit!" he screamed. "Why are fucking autopsies always so god-damn early in the morning?"

A quick wash in the sink and fifteen minutes later, he was pulling into the parking lot of Memorial Hospital. He quickly made his way to the elevator and pressed the down button six times, as if that would make it move any faster. The hospital had also been built into a small hill, and the main entrance put you on the first floor. The morgue was below that. It always made Gideon feel like he was descending into the dungeon. *How appropriate.*

Out of the elevator, a left jog down the short hall, and a quick right to a large, white, heavy door marked with the word "Pathology. He turned the knob slowly, as if to not make a sound, and eased into the room through the partially opened door. The smell hit him first. It was always the smell first. It was a cross between the smell of your garbage cans after they had been sitting outside for three days follow-ing a Thanksgiving Day gorging and the smell of every high school biology class on the day you dissected the little baby pigs.

The room was sterile, totally devoid of color save the urine-tinged yellow tiles along the bottom of the walls. A white plastic bucket sat atop a small table in the corner containing a hacksaw, pruning shears, and the curved stainless steel handle of what Gideon determined was an extremely large kitchen ladle. An assortment of large kitchen knives, filet knives, and a plastic cutting board were carefully laid out along the edge of the steel sink counter. Here we were in the twenty-first century, and the fact of the matter was that the tools of the trade for most MEs were not marvels of modern science and technology, but rather could be purchased at your local hardware store or Bed, Bath & Beyond.

"Morning, Kane, only ten minutes this time . . . you're getting better."

"Back at ya, Doc. How's the meat-packing business treatin' you?"

"I can't complain, and neither can they, I guess," she said, a slight hint of a giggle sneaking through.

Dr. Jernigan stood on a step stool next to the examining table looking over the body of Lindsay Diaz and mumbling into a small steel tape recorder. Covered head to toe in drab blue hospital scrubs, her face covered by a large plastic splash shield, Gideon couldn't make out what she was saying. The doc was an attractive short Irish girl with the requisite pale complexion and long wavy red hair, and as best Gideon could determine through the unflattering blue scrubs, she had a magnificent ass. His friends had told him he needed to move on from Elizabeth, and there was definitely something about Dr. Jernigan that made him a little horny, given the current surroundings. But he just knew that coitus would smell less like sweat and passion and scented oils, and more like that dissection pig from biology class. *Why was it always the smell?* he thought.

"Well, Doc, what are we looking at here?" Gideon asked, staring at her magnificent blue scrubs.

"Quit staring at my ass and look at this," she said. "Your bad guy saved me a little time by doing a modified *Y* incision for me."

The *Y* incision was the standard cut made to facilitate entry into the abdominal cavity, starting at the top of the chest near each shoulder and joining at the area just above the xiphoid process, the breastbone to the layman. From that juncture, a single incision progressed downward toward the bellybutton forming a *Y*. The flaps were then laid open, and the ribs were cut individually, with the aforementioned pruning shears from the white plastic bucket. The ribs and breastbone were then removed in one neat piece in order for the pathologist to examine the organs.

"What about the eyes, Doc?"

"Well, that's another interesting thing, Gideon," she said. She rolled back the right eyelid. In the bright light of the room, Gideon could see a mass of pink flesh behind it.

"Whoa," Gideon exclaimed, "I thought there would just be a hole."

"A common misconception thanks to the horror movie genre," she replied. "When you have an *enucleation*, where the eye is completely removed, the conjunctive tissue behind it fills in the gap. Funny thing here is that whoever did this had some skill. There's very little bleeding, and very little damage to the surrounding tissue."

"A doctor, maybe?" Gideon asked.

"Maybe," Jernigan said.

"What about the stitching over the mouth, Doc?"

"Well, it looks like some kind of monofilament nylon . . . maybe Ethilon."

"What's that used for? Medical?"

"Yeah, sure," said Jernigan. "You could use it for sutures I suppose, but most surgeons nowadays use a Prolene suture. It's harder to work with, but it's stronger than nylon."

"So it's definitely someone with a medical background then?" said Gideon, almost begging for confirmation.

"I don't think so. Here, take a look at this. When most doctors do sutures, their work is almost like a fingerprint, every knot is sort of unique to its creator. The stitching across the lips is a standard crosshatch, but do you see here where the knot is tied off at the left corner of the mouth?"

"Yeah, so?"

"Well, like I said, this is nylon suture, and there's only one throw, or knot, tying off the line."

"And that means . . . ?"

"Well, even the most inexperienced intern knows that a nylon line would require at least four or five throws to give you a secure knot, and here there's only one."

"So maybe he knew she wasn't gonna be moving around enough to break the stitches, so he only needed one?"

"Maybe, but like I said, most sutures are unique, and when you've learned how to do something over and over, it becomes instinctive. You don't consciously make a mistake like this," she said adamantly.

Gideon thought for a moment: *Maybe a doctor. Maybe not a doctor.* Well, that certainly narrows it down.

Jernigan retrieved a small pair of scissors from the counter and began to snip through the individual nylon stitches. Gideon's throat closed slightly, as if he'd just swallowed a big spoonful of peanut butter without any milk. *How could I have overlooked that?* he thought. The missing eyes had made him so preoccupied that he hadn't really taken time to ask why the mouth had been sewn shut. As cold as this room was, he felt a small bead of sweat form on his right temple as Dr. Jernigan released the final stitch from Lindsay's mouth. He just knew what was coming next.

"Nothing," Jernigan said.

"Nothing?"

"Nope, what . . . you thought the eyes would be in here, didn't you? Kane, you're a sick fuck. Remind me not to get on your bad side if you ever decide to go completely postal, huh?"

"You gotta admit," Gideon responded, "it woulda' made a great book, dontcha think?"

Deep down, Gideon had hoped that the eyes *would* be there, if not for the simple fact that he could then chalk this up to a simple fucking whacko with an eyeball fetish who hated women and wanted to hurt them even after death. Now, Gideon thought, he had a complete fucking whacko who hated women, had an agenda, and collected human eyeballs. That meant there would be more.

"Shit, Doc, I'm outta here. I've gotta figure out who she is before this happens again. Call me if you find anything else."

As Gideon walked out into the parking garage, the morning had already become an unbearably muggy ninety degrees. Even with the noxious odor of engine oil and exhaust fumes, it was preferable to the smell of formaldehyde and death. He raised his right shirt sleeve up to his nose and took in the pungent odor of the dissection piggy. It always stuck in your clothes. *Why was it always the smell?* he thought.

6

As Gideon reached the parking lot of the Leon County Sheriff's Office, the old Impala smelled like biology class, but given the temperature outside, rolling the windows down was not an option. The building was fairly new, but for some reason, they had decided to use the same ugly yellow brick that had been used to construct the health department building next door in the early seventies.

Additional floors had been added over the years until now when the sheriff himself could sit in his fourth floor office and gaze out through large tinted glass panes at his domain. Gideon hardly ever went to the fourth floor. It was usually bad if you got called up there, and there were just too many suits and bureaucrats for his liking. Gideon ambled into the lobby, past the "fish bowl," the large glass enclosure behind which usually sat an unexpectedly pleasant receptionist, and over to the elevator beyond. He got in, swiped his ID card, and pressed the control button, only once this time, after all, this was a county elevator, and nothing moved fast in county government. The elevator clamored to life, and seconds later, the door slid open: third floor—Violent Crimes.

As he strode down the dimly lit hallway toward the VCU office, Gideon contemplated the meaning of why the mystery girl had been so badly defiled. He could almost come up with a sick and twisted reason for most of it, but the Y incision bothered him—almost as much as Eddie thinking to check the eyes before he had. Gideon was certain he'd have thought of it eventually.

He walked into the VCU office, a medium-sized room with dull off-white walls and baby-shit green pile carpeting that some consultant had been way overpaid to determine was supposed to be "soothing" and help relieve stress. Six Walmart-quality faux mahogany desks dotted the room in various degrees of helter-skelter. Two of them sat empty, now relegated to a gathering place for misplaced files and assorted crap that nobody wanted on their own desk.

The VCU had once been a team of six detectives, which budget cuts had now reduced to four. In January 2008, the ever astute voting constituency of Florida had approved the governor's property tax relief amendment, and the governor's media relations people had been absolutely brilliant in promoting this brightly colored albatross to the unsuspecting masses. As the rest of the nation was now all too well aware, however, Florida voters had never been too highly acclaimed for fully understanding something prior to punching a chad. What the majority had failed to comprehend was that lower property taxes meant less money in the county coffers. That, in turn, meant fewer firefighters, fewer paramedics, and fewer cops—all of that, for a tax savings that equated to about eleven dollars per month. That apparently was something Floridians felt they could deal with as long as you weren't the one having the heart attack and didn't mind waiting twenty minutes for an ambulance. Or you didn't have a complete and utter sociopath running around your city carving up women like a Christmas ham.

Way to gooo, Florida! Gideon thought as he stood staring at the empty desks.

He plopped down in his chair, head in hands, now staring at the carpet trying to de-stress.

"Not working," he said aloud.

"What's not working?" said a voice from his left.

The voice had come from across the room, and Gideon momentarily snapped away from his happy place long enough to peer over his computer to see Detective Jason Ryden sitting at his desk in the corner, left hand supporting his chin, hunched over, and his face, what Gideon had determined to be, about three inches from the computer screen.

"Who the hell are you talking to anyway?"

"I see dead people," Gideon quipped.

"Yeah, I hate those damn autopsies myself," Jason replied.

Gideon thought for a moment, *Yeah, I'll bet you do. All three of them.*

"You ever notice the smell anymore, Kane?"

Gideon let it go. It wasn't worth the aggravation.

Ryden was the new guy, *the FNG*, in the Violent Crimes Unit, and despite what he thought to the contrary, he would always be the FNG until somebody more FN came along. He was mid to late twenties, athletic, perfect black hair, perfect blue eyes, perfect clothes—perfect, perfect, perfect! Frankly, Gideon thought, his "perfectness" was kind of annoying sometimes. He was what other aging cop veterans, who were losing their hair and growing their waists, would call "pretty." Of course, it was out of jealousy mostly.

Ryden had worked his way through the ranks and into the VCU fairly quickly, and most of the guys thought it was strictly because his daddy worked on the fourth floor. Even Gideon had initially had his reservations when this skinny kid, who didn't even look old enough to *carry* a gun, first reported to the unit after only two years in uniform. Much to everyone's chagrin, however, Ryden had turned out to be a pretty damn good investigator. He had the tools and his looks made people underestimate him (that helped) and he had brains. When he smelled blood, he was a tenacious little son of a bitch. Gideon often thought that he reminded him of him back in the day. That was, of course, before cynicism had grabbed him firmly by the balls and twisted him into submission. *Yeah, well, there was that.*

"What are you working on?" Gideon asked.

"My Facebook page. It's really a pain in the ass to keep it fresh, ya know?"

Gideon winced. "Yeah, I imagine it gets pretty rough."

Gideon lowered his head into his right hand, rubbing his temple and trying to shake off the jackhammer headache that he just knew was inbound. All right, he thought, so maybe he's not *that* much like me.

The door to the VCU flung open, and Eddie hustled over in an obvious caffeine-induced euphoria, an unlit Winston hanging from his mouth, and holding a driver's license photograph of an attractive woman.

"Bingo!" Eddie exclaimed as if the Prize Patrol van had just pulled up outside. He flung the photo onto Gideon's desk.

"Gideon Kane, I would like to introduce you to the lovely Ms. Lindsay Diaz."

"Eddie, you magnificent bastard! How?"

"Yeah I know. It seems our young lady here tried to, unsuccessfully I might add, swipe a four hundred dollar Francesco Biasia shoulder bag from Macy's last summer. The charges were dropped shortly thereafter, however. Her daddy's some rich hot-shit attorney here in town. Anyway, it didn't stick, but the arrest was enough to get her prints in the system and *viola*!"

"Let me get this straight. Her daddy is a rich attorney, and she's shoplifting a bag she could have easily bought with her pop's plastic?"

"Yeah right . . . coz rich people don't steal. Does ENRON ring any bells?" Again, the sarcasm oozed from Eddie's mouth. He continued, easing off just a tad.

"She is . . . sorry, *was* a senior at State, and working on an internship at channel six."

"She's a reporter?" Gideon asked.

"Was," Eddie replied.

"Was?"

"Yeah, *was*. Well, trying to be at least, and Tallahassee police just found her car in the lot at A. J. Henry Park."

TPD was definitely good at nabbing you if you overstayed your parking privileges, Gideon thought.

"CSI is on their way over to process the car," Eddie added.

"So what the hell was she doing at the park? She on a story?"

"Channel six says they didn't send her. Says she was more like a gopher. Program director said he told her to go out and try to scarf up some human interest piece, but he never heard back from her."

Gideon's cell phone buzzed. "Kane . . ."

"Kane, it's Laura Jernigan. The preliminary toxicology screens are back . . . and I found something strange that I think you should see."

"Gimme twenty minutes, Doc," Gideon quipped, closing the phone. Gideon stared down at the carpet again.

"Still not working," he said aloud.

"Eddie, you go to the park. Check on the car, and I'll meet you there later to check around the area.

Eddie nodded and was gone.

Gideon turned to Ryden. "Jason, check with the university. I wanna know about her classes, her boyfriends, sororities, lesbian lovers. I wanna know what kinda toilet paper she wiped her ass with. Got it?"

"Got it."

"And where the hell is Trey?"

"Oh yeah, he called before you got in," Jason said, "He's running late. Something about his daughter eating a clothes pin, or bobby pin . . . bowling pin maybe." Jason's ADD was kicking into high gear. "He said that he'll be in by lunch."

"Fine," Gideon said, already exhausted from the conversation, "When he gets here, tell him to find out what he can about daddy, the hot-shit attorney. I'll be on my cell back at the morgue if anyone needs me."

"Got it."

Gideon hopped off the elevator, hustled down the dogleg hallway, and pushed through the heavy steel door of the pathology lab.

"Whatcha got for me, Doc?" He saw Lindsay Diaz was now lying on the exam table propped up on her left side by a single black rubber block wedged into her lower back above her buttocks. Aided by the effects of full rigor mortis, he thought she looked more like a doll—a mannequin.

"Well, first of all, the preliminary tox screens came back. They show significant concentration of lidocaine in her system, along with elevated levels of epinephrine," said the doctor.

"Lidocaine's an anesthetic, right? So he drugs her so that he has time to do the rest of the damage? Where's the sense in that? Why not just kill her right off the bat? Then he could take his time."

"For someone her size, three hundred fifty milligrams would have been enough to knock her out. The levels of lidocaine in her system were almost twice that. To give you an idea, anything over five hundred and you're flirting with death. The epinephrine levels are quite puzzling though."

"How so?"

Jernigan continued, "During a traditional surgical procedure, the epinephrine would be used in conjunction with the lidocaine as a vasoconstrictor. In other words, it would slow down the bleeding during the procedure. Didn't you say that there wasn't really a lot of blood at the scene?" asked Jernigan.

"Yeah, but again, what the hell for? Why keep her alive during all this if you're just gonna kill her in the end anyway?"

"I don't know. That's your area of expertise, Gideon. But I will tell you this, she died of asphyxiation. I found ordinary white gauze stuffed into both nostrils. A pretty good ways up too, almost into the sinus cavity. It was soaked in lidocaine."

"So . . . with her nose plugged up, and her mouth sewn shut . . . she suffocates," Gideon said.

"Eventually, yes. The anesthetic would have kept her under during the act, but there is the possibility that she may have been, at least . . . semiconscious at some point during the whole ordeal."

Gideon felt the knot growing in the pit of his stomach with the thought that Lindsay may have been aware of what was happening to her.

"Feeling it though," said Jernigan. "I'm not so sure. Look here on her back between the scapulae."

"You couldn't just say shoulder blades?" Gideon quipped.

Gideon bent down slightly, cocking his head to the left, and saw what appeared to be two almost perfectly circular bruises about an inch and a half apart along the center of Lindsay's back, dark purple blending into the yellowish edges.

"X-rays confirm a fracture to the T3 vertabrae, right behind these circular contusions. The bruising is fairly deep, so my guess is she fell backward onto something . . ."

Gideon broke in, "With enough force to break her spine?"

"In a nutshell, yes. There's damage to the spinal cord itself, so it would been very difficult for her to breathe, and there's the distinct possibility that she wasn't able to move once she hit the ground."

Gideon moved closer and noticed a less obvious line of bruising below the circles and running down toward her feet.

"What's this? Lettering or something?" he asked.

"I'm not sure," said Jernigan. "I'll get the lab to take some pictures and blow them up . . . see if there's anything there. I call you as soon as I hear anything."

"Thanks, Doc. Oh, yeah, what about the nylon sutures? Anything more on that?"

"Well, they're not what I'd call surgical grade. I would say sufficient for taxidermy or maybe leatherwork and such. You could probably find it in a hunting or sporting goods store."

"Gee, thanks, that certainly narrows it down," replied Gideon.

The steel door of the lab creaked open. Gideon turned and spied a thin, pale, and balding head peek around the door. The head was attached to a tall, lanky, pale body of a fortyish man who looked older than he should.

"You ready for me, Doc?" said the bald man.

"Almost, Mattie. Just gotta get her pieces back in the shell. Then you can clean up to your heart's content."

"Sounds good, Doc. Mind if I hang out here till you wrap her up?"

"Absolutely," said the doctor. "Gideon, I believe you know Mattie."

"Mattie cleans up after me," she said. "Couldn't do this without him."

"Aww, Dr. Jernigan. Y-y-you flatter me," he stammered.

Gideon's pocket began to vibrate. He pulled out his phone and flipped it open when he saw Eddie's number.

"Gimme good news, Eddie," said Kane.

"Sorry, bubba, not today. The car's clean. Just a few books and some spoiled take-out food, standard college kid's fare. We'll tow it back to the lab and check it for trace later today, but I wouldn't get your hopes up. I'll wait for you here so we can walk the area."

"Drivin' time from the hospital, Eddie."

The elevator shuddered as it reached the first floor. Strange, he hadn't really noticed the smell this time, he thought. The doors slid open, and Gideon stepped out into the atrium.

"Trey?" Gideon asked.

Trey Morris stopped and turned toward Gideon, his five-year-old, Sarah, draped sleepily over his shoulder. Trey looked tired.

"How's she doing?" Gideon asked.

"Well, the human vacuum cleaner here swallowed a pin. The kind with the little plastic ball thingie on one end?"

"I'm not even gonna ask how, Trey. She gonna be okay?"

"The doctor says in technical terms, the pointy end is facing backward, and that we're just gonna have to wait for it to do its own thing."

"Ouch!"

"Yeah, tell me about it. Nothing like checking your child's stool on the hour to remind you why you became a parent."

Trey—Gideon's best friend. He was tall, yet not imposing as most people who are taller than you seem to appear. In his late thirties, he was balding well beyond his years. The "skin insula" he would call it, where your hair turns in a full frontal retreat toward your ass, leaving behind a lonely thin strip down the center grasping desperately for your forehead.

Pleasantly plump, he would refer to himself. As no one else before, Gideon had not met a man so comfortable in his own skin. If you were a righteous man, Trey was your best friend. If you were on the wrong side of things, well, let's just say you didn't want to go down that road with the man. And then there was the "it" factor. Trey had it. Everything Gideon had once coveted: loving wife, loving family—apparent happiness, not to mention furniture.

Gideon turned toward the garage entrance. "We had a good one last night, Trey. I know you're busy, but I could really use you on this one."

"Let me get her home to Sherrell, and I'll get up to the office."

"Great, I gotta run, but Jason will fill you in on the details when you get there."

7

Mathias sat at the old wooden desk in his room rapping the pencil against the desktop as he ignored the homework in front of him, staring out the lone window. The lone majestic picture of the Virgin Mary stared down at him from the wall above as the only form of decoration in the otherwise unobtrusive room—no posters of Twisted Sister, no baseball gloves, no dirty clothes piled high in the corner. Other than a glass container of marbles, there was no sign that a teenager dwelled within. The faint sounds of *Lola* by the Kinks barely displaced the busy sounds from the street outside. While the other kids flocked to the new bands like Poison and Motley Crue, he preferred the older stuff. The year, 1983, had been a sheltered existence for him, as had all the previous ones in his short time on earth. Mother didn't want her baby boy turning into a hoodlum, she would say. Like any other eighteen-year-old, he would have happily broken the volume knob at ultrasonic, but his mother didn't approve of such music. He didn't dare play it loud enough for her to hear.

He could still smell Debbie Finch on his clothes. He noticed a dark red spot on his left shirt sleeve. Mother would be upset if she saw that, he thought, but how could she when she had watched him perform so magnificently. Little Debbie had never seen it coming—the knife sliding effortlessly across her throat, even while in the midst of the most indecent of acts. The dim kitchen light glinted off the crimson liquor that flowed down her chest as her eyes stared up at him in disbelief. He had seen Mother at the door and knew what had to come next. As her dying body gave way to the floor, he had reached out, grabbing Debbie by the hair and pulled her head away from him, tucking and zipping as he moved. He dragged her toward the kitchen and out the back door. As he looked back toward the hall for her, his only thought was that Mother would make him clean up the mess before he went to bed. As he lay in bed that night, he recalled Mother coming home from bridge and standing, for a bit, in the doorway to his room. He felt her staring for what seemed an eternity. She liked to watch. Then he felt her lips on his forehead.

"Good night, child," she whispered, her lips moving down to his, uncomfortable at first, then giving way to acquiescence. He felt her hand as she pulled back the sheet, cold against his leg, as his eyes slackened shut.

He awoke the next morning as the sun shone through the window. Billy Graham echoed from the Zenith downstairs as the smell of bacon wafted into the room. He slowly descended the stairs and meandered down the hallway toward the kitchen. Mother stood over the stove paying him no attention as he slumped into a chair at the table.

"Good morning, child," she said. "Sleep well?"

"Yes, Mother, thank you."

"Some eggs, child? You need your strength, you know. What with your cavorting with the tramps and all."

"Please, Mother. And I would hardly call it cavorting really. More of a romp or even a frolic," he replied.

"You're dirty," she said. "I can smell her on you."

Mathias leaned over his plate of eggs, tuning out Mother, *L-O-L-A. Lola* playing over and over in his head. Mother would drone on for another ten minutes on his "unhealthy" obsession with girls, about how *she* and the Blessed Virgin herself should rightfully be the only women in his life, and how one should always cant the knife downward at a forty-five-degree angle when slicing in order to sever the jugular and the vocal chords in one swift motion. Blah blah blah!

Why was she always so critical? he thought. After all, she had taught him well, and he had been a most adept student.

"Mathias!" her shrill voice breaking through the veil of disinterest he had created. "Have you been listening to a thing I've said?"

"Of course, Mother," he mumbled.

"Good. Then it's time for you to go finish cleaning up your mess before she ripens."

Mathias pushed away from the table, head hung down, reflecting his displeasure, as would any boy who had just been forced to complete his household chores. He ambled out the back kitchen door and into the rear yard and made his way to the old wooden toolshed.

As he swung open the frail door, the pungent odor of decay struck him squarely in the face as he spied the lifeless remains of li'l Debbie lying in a crumpled heap on the dirt floor, a pool of crimson mud forming a halo on the ground beneath her head. Grabbing her by the arms, he slung her up into the wheelbarrow. As he struggled to push out of the dark, dank shed, the morning's heat became readily apparent. He wheeled around the rear of the shed and pointed toward the wood line that butted up against the rear of the property, then onto a footpath that he had carved out himself over the years trekking down to fish at the banks of the Wakulla River. It was peaceful here in the woods with the birds singing, the sound of the river creeping by, the smell of jasmine in the air, and all manner of small creatures flittering around. He came here often to think—to get away—sometimes from Mother's incessant lecturing.

He stopped short at the end of the path, put the wheelbarrow down, and walked out into the clearing and into the open bank. A small flats boat eased downriver and into view from his left, only yards away. An elderly man wearing a fly-fishing vest and a crinkled boonie cap waved as he tooled by, oblivious. Mathias waved back and waited until the old man cleared the bend, out of sight, and walked confidently back to his prize. Mathias eased the wheelbarrow out into the bank and into the cold murky water. Tilting it to the right, Debbie Finch slipped effortlessly beneath the surface. Wide expanses of mud from the river bottom made the water silty and impenetrable to the eye. The current at the surface was swift and would carry her the rest of the way downstream, assuming that she didn't get snagged up under some tree branches and logs which lined the banks of this section of the river. And even if she did, the alligators would happen upon her soon enough. He watched for a bit as she slowly drifted away just below the surface and around the bend.

Mathias made his way back up to the house, stopping to place the wheelbarrow back in the shed. The river water had rinsed the blood away, and he scraped the dirt from the dry part of the floor, covering the halo. As he walked up the steps to the house, he pulled off his wet shoes, his favorite red Chuck Taylors, pulled out the tongues, and placed them neatly on the stoop to dry in the sun. As he walked into the kitchen, the house no longer smelled of bacon and breakfast but rather the acrid odor of bleach and disinfectant. The breakfast dishes had already been put away, and he could see the wet circular pattern on the rug down the hall where Mother had attempted to erase the last vestiges of Ms. Finch.

"Mother?" he yelled.

There was no answer. Some writing on a small white napkin caught his eye on the kitchen table:

Mathias,

I have gone to the grocery to purchase more bleach. Your indiscretions, lately, have become quite costly. Upon my return, we shall discuss how you may make reparations to me.

Love,

Mother

Just as he'd finished reading the salutation came the knock at the front door. He looked upward and down the hallway, and through the glass, he could see the uniformed man standing on the other side and the familiar and ultimately recognizable star on his chest. Mathias's eyes darted to the wet spot on the rug and then back to the door. The man knocked again, harder this time, cupping his hand to shade his eyes as he now peered through the glass, looking directly at him. *How could they have gotten here so fast?* he thought. No one knew she was coming. He had slipped the note to meet him inside her pocket as they had left class, and he had waited behind the diner as it had instructed. He'd even signed it "Anonymous" in case anyone else had come upon it. If she showed, great; if she didn't, no big deal. No tracks to cover. How could they have known?

"Son," the deputy said, "I really need you to open this door now. Do you understand me?"

Mathias, again, glanced back at the spot on the rug—unable to move.

8

Gideon pushed through the door of the VCU, passed Ryden on the phone, and straight to his computer. He thought about all the different injuries, what they all meant, and why they had all been brought together on Lindsay Diaz. He googled "Mouth Sewn Shut" and was bombarded by page after page of a hard-core punk band by the same name. No help there.

Ryden stopped talking for a moment, cupping his hand over the phone.

"Gideon, I've got the boyfriend on the phone. Says he hasn't been able to get hold of Lindsay for a couple of days, and then he saw the news story. He called us to find out if it was her. What do I tell him?"

"Tell him we need to talk, and soon," said Gideon.

Gideon's eyes went back to the computer monitor. *There's a reason for all of it*, he thought, *but what?* He thought about all the cliches about eyes that he could remember: about the eyes being the key to the soul or that beauty is in the eye of the beholder—it still didn't make any sense.

Jason clicked off the phone. "Boyfriend's a Ronnie Shaw. Says he's gotta go to work, but we can come talk to him there before the dinner rush. He's a bartender at Fusion down off Monroe Street."

"Does he sound like he knows anything?" asked Gideon.

"He sounds like a frat boy who isn't all that concerned about his *girlfriend du jour* if you know what I mean. Didn't seem upset enough to me."

"Sounds like as good a place as any to start," said Gideon. Besides, Fusion had a lobster ravioli that made his stomach growl every time he drove by the place.

Gideon's phone buzzed, and he saw Eddie's number on the caller ID. "Shit! Eddie, I'm sorry dude, I got sidetracked on some stuff from the ME's office, and I completely forgot. I'll leave right now. I can be there in ten."

"Oh, that's okay. I really enjoy traipsing around through tick-in-fested woods in this heat looking for God know's what!" Eddie said.

"Well, did you find anything?"

"Yeah! Actually I did!"

"And?"

"Say, pretty please."

"Eddie! Goddamnit! What did you find?"

"All right already, you don't have to get snippy. Down by the ravine, we found a piece of leather, like a strap for something. Also found a scrap of paper with some writing on it, says 'A. J. Henry eight o'clock.'"

"So she was there to meet someone?" Gideon asked.

"Looks that way. If it's hers, that is. Doesn't look like it's been here that long. There's also what looks like blood on a rock down here. I'll send it all to trace and see if we can get something from any of it."

Gideon closed the phone and leaned back in his chair. If Lindsay was there to meet someone and that someone killed her, then her friends or family would have to know something. An attractive twenty-something woman did not just walk into the woods at sunset to meet a complete stranger. What he couldn't quite wrap his head around was that if this was someone who actually knew her, someone she was comfortable enough to meet, how could this someone do these things to her? Extremely violent homicides were usually reserved for relatives, acquaintances, lovers, and such. It was easy to take a gun and shoot someone, especially in today's society. But to get up close and personal, that takes rage, not just anger—and a lot of it. The kind of rage that takes time to manifest and grow, layer upon layer, until it erupts into complete and utter destruction. Marriage, for instance, was a perfect facilitator for such happenings, but there was no indication thus far that Lindsay Diaz was married.

And then, of course, you have the sociopath, which kinda throws a wrench into that whole theory. A true sociopath has no conscience. He knows what's right and what's wrong—he just doesn't give a shit. Tallahassee was all too familiar with this type of evil. Gideon was still a boy in January of 1978 when Ted Bundy crept into the Chi Omega sorority house and forever thrust the city into the annals of whack-job history. And nearly thirty years later, when the city believed it had finally put enough time between itself and Chi Omega, along came Gary Michael Hilton—a case Gideon and his team had become intimately involved in. Hilton had kidnapped, tortured, and killed several women throughout the southeast during his spree: a schoolteacher in nearby Crawfordville, a young student in southern Georgia, not to mention a plethora of unsolved homicides that varying agencies suspected him of committing. And what else did these two pieces of shit have in common? They both got caught. They made enough mistakes—lost enough control that they left themselves as vulnerable as their victims. And that is where the members of the VCU spent their lives: in that small and scary place looking for tiny mistakes in the dark. To capture pure evil, one must be surrounded by it, to think like it, and to anticipate it.

Gideon looked up at Ryden who was pecking away at his keyboard.

"Jason, did you find out anything about her connection to the university?" he asked.

"Yeah, she was finishing up hers last semester. Due to get a communications degree here in a couple of months. Last class she took in her major was some kind of investigative journalism deal she finished about a month ago. This semester was just the internship, plus some electives to get her total hours up so she could graduate at the end of the summer."

"What about the job at the television station?" asked Gideon.

"TV station says she was interning as part of her final semester. She hadn't been there very long, so nobody could really tell me a whole lot," Ryden said.

"Find out who she reported to at the station. Someone had to be signing off on her intern paperwork so that she would get credit. That's who we wanna talk to."

"I'm on it, boss."

Trey pushed through the door with the look of a dead man on his last walk.

"You look like shit," said Ryden.

Trey replied, "Yeah, well shit looks like you."

"What the hell does that mean?" Gideon said.

"I dunno . . . cut me some slack. Huh, I've been sitting over a toilet with a colander for the last few hours."

Trey poured himself a cup of three-hour-old coffee and plunked down at his desk, swinging his feet up onto the corner. "So what do we got?" he said.

Gideon tossed the ME's report onto Trey's desk. "Jason will fill you in on the other details when you're done going through this," he said. "I'm off to see an old friend."

Gideon jumped into the Impala and cruised out onto Pensacola Street, up Ocala Road, and onto Tennessee Street. Driving through 600 Block, he reminisced about his own pre-cynical college days—too many late nights at Bullwinkle's Tavern, spinning the free drink wheel at Poor Paul's Pourhouse, concerts at Floyd's Music Store, convincing a nubile and slightly intoxicated young coed that you were the drummer (it was simple, it was easy; besides nobody could ever see the drummer's face anyway), etc. And now, nearly twenty years later, a new generation of substance-craving college kids poured in and out of his same old haunts from back in the day—including Lindsay Diaz. Only difference was: he'd lived through his depravity.

Gideon sailed down Mahan Drive, catching all the green lights, an amazing feat anytime of the day, let alone in the early afternoon. And he was pleased enough to smile, which he rarely did anymore. Lillian Langdale's place was almost right across the street from the state headquarters of the Florida Department of Law Enforcement. He had actually been the FNG eleven years ago on his first big burglary case. He was delivering some fingerprints that he had personally retrieved from his first major burglary to the lab at FDLE when he first noticed the sign across the street:

Madame Langdale

Psychic

The huge sign seemed closer to the road than any of the others, light blue, with a big white hand, fingers outstretched. It sort of reminded him of Mickey Mouse's hand, and he chuckled every time he'd gone by since. But that day was different. He was proud of the latent prints he'd been able to recover, and being new and somewhat naïve, he figured the lab would be able to simply put them into its computer and spit out the name of the bad guy, just like on TV. When the technician told him that the prints weren't of sufficient quality—which they liked to say instead of "You suck at taking prints"—he was devastated. He literally had no leads, and there was no way he was "cold casing" his first major. On his way back to the office, he thought to himself that it couldn't hurt. He pulled into the parking lot—a very nondescript building of white stucco, crumbling in places, and the baby blue roof to match the sign out front.

He would never forget as he opened the heavy oaken door for the first time the bright sunlight outside blinding him as he stepped into the very dark sitting room. Candles flickered and shadows bounced around as his eye's adjusted to the dark. The walls were a darker blue, and a pair of blood red velvet curtains separated another unseen place.

"Hello?" he mumbled, turning his back to the curtain. His eyes were not cooperating, and he blinked frequently, struggling to find, perhaps, a window. He was a cop, had been one for years, and he'd rarely ever been scared. Uneasy, yes, but not scared. This place, however, gave him the creeps.

"Good afternoon," came a voice from behind him.

Gideon was so startled, he remembered, that he spun around and drew his gun halfway out of the holster before catching himself.

"I am Madame Langdale," she said.

He eased his gun back into the holster and saw a woman, fif-tyish, wearing a yellow-flowered housecoat, curlers in her jet-black hair, and a Marlboro Red hanging from the corner of her mouth.

"Geez, lady! You should really not sneak up on people like that. I could have shot you!" Gideon snapped.

"I knew you would not . . . of course," she replied.

He felt a grin forming on his face, and he tried to contain it, her accent reminiscent of part Bela Lugosi and part Russian countess. Polish maybe, he thought, but definitely from over there somewhere.

"I'm sorry," he said, "you're just not what I expected."

"What?" she replied. "I should walk out here in a black robe with a red velvet lampshade on my head?"

"Well . . . yeah, actually," he said.

She walked him into the rear parlor behind the red velvet curtains and motioned him to sit at a large, round mahogany table decorated with triangular patterns of lighter wood diverging at the center. He had been skeptical, but they sat for an hour, talking and drinking Earl Grey. He explained to her about his first major case that had no leads, and she explained to him how he already knew the answer to his own questions, he just needed to listen to his inner voice more often—a typical tactic used by bogus psychics. But she didn't feel that way to him. He wasn't exactly sure, at first, if she was full of shit or not, but he knew he kind of liked the old lady for some reason. She had, after all, been the one that had told him that he would meet Elizabeth the day before he had been to Tom Clower's office. There was the part, however, where she failed to advise him that she would eventually move on without him, leaving his life in a pathetic heap he could only hope would aspire to become shambles someday.

Yeah, there was that.

Despite the inauspicious start to their relationship, Gideon genuinely came to like the old woman, even to trust her more than he trusted most people, which wasn't much at all. After she'd been dead on about Liz, he'd drop by once in a while and talk about his cases, not really to get any big psychic revelations, but more to vent. Lillian Langdale became somewhat of a therapist to Gideon. While she sometimes talked in circles, he came to appreciate that she would just listen to him talk, especially after the breakup. She in turn enjoyed the polite conversations over a pleasant cup of tea and the company. Gideon had often wondered how she could afford to stay open, seeing as how he had never seen another client whenever he dropped by. But she *was* a psychic, he thought. Maybe she picked the lottery numbers or something, and this was just a side gig to keep her entertained. In any event, she was always a good friend. And what he needed now was answers—answers that he was sure only Lillian could produce.

Gideon pulled the Impala into the parking lot, got out, and walked up to the door, grabbing the handle and closing his eyes for a few seconds before going in. Lillian had thoughtfully instructed him to do this after his first visit in order to avoid any unnecessary gunfire. He walked through the outer sitting room and brushed aside the velvet curtain. Lillian sat at the table, playing solitaire with deck of cards in a haunted house motif.

"How is that any fun for you?" Gideon said.

"What do you mean? A lot of people play solitaire," she replied.

"Yeah, but a lot of people who play solitaire aren't psychics. Shouldn't you already know if you're gonna win or not?"

"You know something?" Lillian said. "You're a real pain my ass sometimes."

Gideon smiled and sat down across the table from her. Lillian continued playing, never looking up from the table, the all too familiar cigarette hanging from her mouth.

"You know those things are gonna kill you some day, right?" he said.

"Did you come here to bust my balls," she said in her best Count Dracula accent, "or do you have something substantial to contribute to the forthcoming conversation? I will not break out the good tea unless I am stimulated."

"I've got a dead woman with her eyes removed and her mouth sewn shut."

The cigarette fell from Lillian's mouth. Without looking up, she stood, scooting the chair back with her legs, and walked around to the small kitchenette behind her.

"For this, I'll break out the Darjeeling. It's first flush, and quite mild," she said. She placed the kettle on the stove, turned around, and fell back against the counter. She felt light-headed, and her hands gripped tightly on the oven door behind her.

"You okay?" Gideon asked. "You look pale, even in this light."

"Are you familiar with paganism, Gideon?"

"It's basically a bunch of people running around naked in the woods, lighting fires, and praying to the Norse god, Odin, right?"

"No, not so much," she said. "Paganism is a term created by the Christian church to encompass many different religions outside the realm of Judaism and Christianity. The Jews refer to them as gentiles. Essentially, the word pagan has come to mean heathen or non-Christian. What I do here would be considered pagan, even today, by the Catholic Church."

"I don't follow," said Gideon as his brow wrinkled.

"Let me give you an example you might be more familiar with," Lillian said. "In the late sixteen hundreds, hundreds of women were burned at the stake as witches, accused of performing the black arts."

"Okaaayy," Gideon said, "so you're saying I've got witches running amok around Tallahassee. Lillian, do you hear yourself?"

"No, Gideon, listen! Many of the Wiccan rituals required that a blood sacrifice be offered. The eyes and mouth of the sacrifice were often sealed shut to prevent the soul from leaving during the ceremony so that the mind, body, and soul could be kept together and intact for whatever gods or demons that they worshipped."

Gideon felt his throat swell and dry. "You are," he stammered, "you're saying that I've got witches running around town! Flying monkeys and all that! But wait a minute, her eyes weren't sewn shut. They were actually removed. Doesn't that throw a kink into your theory?"

"Gideon, have you ever heard the term, 'the eyes are the window to the soul'? The eyes are sealed during the rite, but it would stand to reason that if that saying is true, once the ritual was over and the sacrifice complete . . ."—she hesitated—"Gideon, by sealing the mouth, the soul would seek out the eyes as a means of escaping the torment that the body had endured, and by removing the eyes, the person performing the ritual might believe that they're taking possession of that person's soul."

"Jesus Christ!" Gideon howled.

"Not so much really," Lillian replied wryly. "Pretty much the other guy," she said, never taking her eyes off of the floor.

Gideon continued in a lower, yet no less hurried tone, "So what, pray tell, would these witches do, exactly, with this soul?"

"It could be any manner of conjurings. There are hundreds of different rituals that require a sacrifice to some entity or another, all with different desired outcomes. Resurrection, maybe?" she said.

"Let me get this straight," he said, the sarcasm dripping from his mouth, "I'm looking for a witch . . . who brutally murders people . . . then steals their eyes . . . so that he can bring back *other* dead people. Does that about cover it?"

"Gideon, you're missing the point," she replied, her patience wearing thin, "It doesn't even have to be a witch! As a matter of fact, modern-day Wiccans do not entirely embrace the notion of resurrection. Actually, the Catholic Church does more than anyone to facilitate the concept than any other religion or philosophy. Don't you remember anything from when you were an altar boy? Modern witches follow a philosophy that believes that every person has the right to follow their own path to spirituality, so long as that path does not bring harm to others."

"So then what are we talking about here, Lillian?"

"My best guess," she continued, "is that you have an extremely disturbed son of a bitch with an extensive background in Christianity . . . or a crazy altar boy . . . one of the two."

Gideon stood speechless for a moment, never dropping his gaze at Lillian.

"Ya know something?" he quipped. "You never told me what you used to do before this gig."

The right corner of Lillian's mouth drew slightly inward forming a devious half-smile.

"I dabbled," she said, "a little of this and a little of that. Now come, we must drink this tea before it gets too cold."

"Maybe another time. You've got my head going in a thousand different directions now, and I've got to check some things out."

Gideon grabbed her by the face and kissed her on the forehead softly, as you would your elderly grandmother. Lillian had become that to him: the only woman in his life who had maintained any semblance of constancy. Normalcy, certainly not—but constancy nonetheless.

As he reached the door, grabbing for the handle, he stopped for a moment and turned back toward her, the look of an ego-crushed adolescent boy washing over his face.

"About Liz . . . will she?" he said.

Lillian sensed what he needed answers to.

"If she remains in your heart, child, then she was never really gone."

God I hate when she does that shit! he thought, then smiled and walked outside.

9

The public library was just a short drive away from Lillian Langdale's place, out on Park Avenue downtown, almost directly across the street from Elizabeth's office. He found a parking spot in front of the federal courthouse and tossed the Sheriff's: Official Business placard on the dash. Since 9/11, you couldn't leave a car anywhere near a government building in this town unless you were the cops. As he stepped out of the car, he looked back over his shoulder toward the second story window of the old red brick building across the street. It was what was left of the original architecture from the thirties, a new high-rise hotel swallowing it up from next door. He could see Liz hunched over her desk, as she was most often, poring over paperwork. *Busy as usual*, he thought. Suddenly, he saw that she'd stopped and sat up as if someone had called her. She looked around for a moment, shook her head, and resumed her hunch over the desk. Gideon smiled. They'd always had that kind of connection. She had sensed something, and that something was him.

"It ain't over yet, baby," he whispered aloud.

He flipped the keys in his hand, still smiling, and walked down the street toward the library.

He walked quickly up the steps, glancing at his watch, and passed by the white concrete columns and up onto the red brick entrance of the building. As he pulled open the glass door, the rush of cold air blasted against him as he entered. It was ridiculously hot outside, which he had realized even during the short jaunt down the street, and this would be a welcome respite. Gideon walked into the foyer and spied a young woman behind the desk stamping books: mid-twenties, long jet-black hair tied up in back with a red velvet scrunchie. Her large-framed glasses accentuated her bright green eyes as she looked up at him, smiling. A very modest black Ann Taylor suit with notched lapels and a four-button front, a red silk stretch collared blouse protruding from underneath. Judging by the length at which the twins were poking out from between the lapels, Gideon was positive that she had purchased the suit prior to some upper body enhancement. Beyond that, however, she looked demure, he thought. She was attractive, in a bookish sort of way. Gideon felt himself staring. She looked up at him and smiled, dropping her gaze back down to the stack of books before her. It had been years since Gideon had been in a library or with another woman for that matter, but this was definitely not at all how he remembered librarians look. She was neither stuffy, nor stodgy, nor old. There were no visible moles and no horn-rimmed glasses connected by a chain. Quite to the contrary, all this led to the misbegotten, exclusively male belief that this woman was a raving maniac in bed. Gideon pictured Sharon Stone without the icepick. Years of practice and study had made him quite astute in these matters. He approached the desk and thought, *Aww, honey, if only she hadn't beaten you to me, we'd be knockin' the Dewey decimals off the shelves right now.*

"Hello," she whispered. Her voice was soft and raspy, and he found himself wanting to ask where the *Kama Sutra* was located, hoping she might get the hint and perhaps want to go somewhere for a nine-dollar cup of coffee and discuss positions 120–140.

"Resurrection?" Gideon asked, feeling himself sweating for the first time.

"Excuse me?" she said, her face blanching to white, a slight smile forming as she fidgeted with the scrunchie.

"Resurrection," he repeated, "where would I find books on that?"

"Ohhh, I'm sorry," she said giggling. "That's not what I thought you said."

Puzzled, Gideon stared for a moment then smirked, realizing the alliteration had not been lost on her.

She pointed to a stack near the west staircase as her devious smile overtook him. Gideon nodded his appreciation as he quickly moved away from the desk and suddenly realizing that he had actually been aroused, taking care that his front was facing away from her.

Browsing through the stacks, Gideon realized that there weren't a lot of books on the subject that didn't have to do with being reborn. He had always thought that that was just something one did in prison. He spent the next hour leafing through countless texts on pagan rituals, the evolution of witchcraft, and the history of the pentagram—nothing very helpful. He stood up from the reading table, last book in hand, and placed it back on the shelf. As he did so, his eye caught the spine of an unmarked book, three to the right, and pulled it from the shelf. *The Lesser Key of Solomon* was etched in gold print across the brown leather cover, while *The Book of Sigils* was emblazoned on the inside. *Absolutely nothing helpful,* he thought. Gideon looked at his watch just as the cell buzzed in his pocket, and he recognized Ryden's number.

"What's up, Jason?"

"I'm on my way over to meet with the boyfriend. Thought you might wanna go with me," he answered.

"Meet you there in a few."

Gideon stood, leaving the books he'd been leafing through on the reading table, save the odd leather book, which he tucked instinctively under his arm and walked quickly toward the front doors without thinking.

"Sir!" the voice called from the direction of the front desk.

Gideon turned toward her as she motioned him over. Then the notion hit him.

"Oh, I apologize," he said. "I just got a call about a really important meeting, and I just got sidetracked. I really was gonna check it out."

"No, sir, that's okay. People do it all the time," she said.

"Please don't call me sir. My name is Gideon."

"Actually, I think I might have found the book that you were looking for," she continued. "It just came back in, and I haven't had a chance to put it back out in the stacks. Wait here just a moment."

As she turned away from him and walked back toward the office, he couldn't help realizing that there might be something to that phrase about being able to bounce a quarter off of something or other. At the moment, his concentration was lax. He quickly shifted his gaze upward as she returned and slid a brown paper bag across the desk.

"Well, actually," he said, "I don't think have a library card."

"That's okay. I won't tell if you won't," she whispered, her lips pursed.

At that instant, his cell phone buzzed again. He pulled it from his pocket and saw Jason's number.

"I'm leaving the library now!" he yelled, snapping the phone shut. An elderly woman sitting at a nearby table reading the day's newspaper froze his gaze and gave him a look of utter contempt.

Staring back at her, he said glibly, "What, you couldn't spring for the fifty cents to buy your own?"

Gideon turned back toward the desk, picked the paper bag up, and stuck it snug up under his arm with the first.

"Thanks for this," he said, "I'll get them back to you as soon as I can."

"Please do," she said smiling.

Gideon turned and walked quickly out the front door and onto the cobblestone street. As he walked toward the Impala, curiosity grabbed him. He hadn't thought to look or ask. He stopped momentarily and pulled the book partially from the bag: *The Kama Sutra*. Gideon smiled and pulled a small piece of paper that was sticking out from beneath the cover: "Call me - Stephanie 385-7816."

He laughed, slid the book back into the bag, and continued walking back toward the car with a significantly new bounce in his step. As he opened the car door, he tossed the book onto the front passenger seat and felt a chill. As he turned, he glanced up at the window across the street, just in time to see Liz turn quickly back around toward her desk.

"Detective Kane?" came a voice from below his gaze.

Gideon glanced down and saw the pallid, rawboned man sitting on the park bench gnawing on a sandwich of some kind in front of Elizabeth's office. His brown herringbone driving cap was pulled low, obscuring his face, an odd martini glass-shape adorning the top. As Gideon eased closer, he noted the white, short-sleeved, button-down shirt, brushed khakis, and light brown Wolverine work boots with plenty of heavy dark spatter on them.

Blood?

As the realization traveled along the neural pathways of his brain, he instinctively reached his right hand up to his hip, grasping the forty-five caliber Glock pistol at his side as a chill ran up him.

"Do I know you?" Gideon asked.

With his unladen right hand, the man tipped the bill of his cap back looking up at him, and he suddenly snapped back into reality.

"Mattie, right?" said Gideon. "From the morgue."

"Correct, sir," Mattie said. "Been to the library, I see?"

"Yep, doing a little research on a case I'm working."

"That girl in the lab this morning, is it?"

Gideon couldn't quite place Mattie's accent, suffice to say somewhere between a leprechaun and an Amish schoolteacher.

"What are you doing here?" Gideon asked.

"Just enjoying the view," he replied. "Just enjoying the view."

View? Gideon thought.

"Well, listen, Mattie," Gideon said hurriedly, "I gotta run, but it was good to see you."

Expressionless, Mattie waved the sandwich at Gideon as he turned away and made for the Impala. He watched as Gideon sped away down Park Avenue and disappeared around the corner at Adams Street. He looked upward toward the red brick building to his right.

"Yes . . . quite the view," he whispered aloud.

10

Abigail Arbin backed the 1974 Plymouth Valiant from the driveway, hands at ten and two. She slowly eased away from the home, eastward down the winding gravel road and toward the river bridge, which would take her into town. Peering through her brown, square, horn-rimmed glasses, she fumbled with the radio knob until Beethoven's "Symphony No. 6" crept through the single monotone speaker. Her father had loved Beethoven. The only daughter of a priggish school-teacher, Abigail had grown up under her father's ever watchful eye as an outwardly prim and proper young lady. Her mother had not survived the childbirth, and she felt that her father had never quite forgiven her for that. Virtue and religious devotion had been instilled into every facet of her mostly puritanical upbringing. So at seven-teen, when she had become pregnant with Mathias, he cast her aside like so much garbage. Abigail knew it was more for appearances than his disdain for unwedded fornication. After all, she often thought, it would have been mighty hypocritical of him. Openly, he would quote Romans 8:17 which said: "Because the carnal mind is enmity against God . . . So then they that are in the flesh cannot please Him."

She remembered all the days of his sanctimonious preaching about righteousness, devotion, reverence, and immorality. She had *also* remembered all the nights that he crept silently into her room as she lay sleeping. She too remembered the appropriate Bible pas-sage that would come to define her existence in Matthew 7:17 which states: "Even so every good tree bringeth forth good fruit; but a cor-rupt tree bringeth forth evil fruit."

Abigail had kept the pregnancy a secret as long as she could, and when it was no longer possible, she moved away to raise a son—alone. She had returned to Tallahassee when Mathias was three. Her father having passed a year earlier, she told anyone who asked, simply, that the baby's father had been killed fighting in Vietnam—a hero. To Abigail, the concept of death had become the supreme disinfectant; the ultimate method for sanitizing one's inadequacies and indiscretions—a trait that she had, intentionally or not, passed on to her son.

The Bradfordville Store was only a few miles from the house, and Abigail lost herself in the pastoral tones of the symphony piping through the radio, her concentration lost on the task at hand.

The fully loaded pulpwood truck was traveling westbound toward the Bradfordville Store, hauling an off-highway load of about 120,000 pounds of freshly cut timber. Headed for the St. Joe Paper Company, the driver was still at least an hour away and running behind. The smaller back roads would provide a shortcut if he could keep it on the road, he thought. The winding back roads proved more than tricky, trying to compensate for the overloaded trailer that was weighted too heavily to the rear. Rounding the blind curve, he spied the bridge and the powder blue Plymouth approaching from the other side. Not quickly enough, he realized the load had shifted and felt the trailer slide out beside him, the weight of the timber crashing through the aging bridge supports. As the bridge gave way, he last saw the nose of the Valiant pointing straight down into the river before disappearing beneath the sixty tons of debris. Fleeting glimpses of powder blue and the crumpled license plate were all that was visible through the smoke and dust.

It had taken an hour for the troopers to reach the wreckage at the bottom of the ravine. They had been able to identify the Plymouth's owner from the plate and asked the sheriff to send a deputy to the house to confirm. It would be another three hours before they reached Abigail Arbin beneath three feet of roiling river water.

Mathias stood in the kitchen frozen, his eyes locked on the deputy through the glass.

"Son, come open the door, please!"

Without realizing, he moved slowly down the hallway in a fog. He saw the movement of the deputy's mouth but heard nothing. His world was dark, closing in around him, as he moved through the tunnel and into the light. He flicked open the lock and turned the handle, opening the door just a crack.

His voice crackling, Mathias asked, "Can I help you?"

The deputy stood motionless for a moment, and Mathias saw that he was tall yet stocky, with a large, stoic face and a flattop haircut. A chrome long-barreled revolver hung from a low holster on his right hip, the black leather strap of a slapjack protruding from his back pocket. Buck Blackstock had already been a cop for a long time in nineteen eighty-three, but these moments never got any easier regardless of how long you'd been doing the job.

"Son, does anyone here drive a blue Plymouth?" he asked.

"Sure," Mathias responded, his voice still crackling. "Mother just left a little while ago for the store. She should be back any time now. I would ask you in to wait, but Mother doesn't take well to strangers in the house when she's away. Perhaps you could come back later?"

"Son, is your mother Abigail Arbin?"

"Why yes, she is. Is something the matter with Mother?"

As Buck Blackstock launched into the standard "I'm sorry for your loss" monologue, Mathias felt his legs gave way, and he dropped to the floor in the open doorway, his eyes focused on the muddied boots of the deputy. All sound had dropped away, and Mathias felt as if he'd just been rapped in the head with that slapjack. Surprisingly, to him, the thoughts of Mother quickly gave way to relief. The realization struck him oddly.

They're not here for the girl! he thought.

The deputy leaned over, and Mathias grabbed his arm as he pulled himself to his feet. Deputy Blackstock entered the doorway and walked Mathias over to a cherry wooden sitting bench in the hall. He backed up a bit and stood centered on the hallway rug directly above Debbie Finch's final resting place. He felt the moistness of the carpet beneath his feet and momentarily lifted his left foot, looking for the spot. Mathias felt a knot growing in his stomach as Blackstock looked back upward at him.

He knows! Mathias thought.

"I apologize," said the deputy. "I must have tracked some mud in here from the riverbank. If you have a towel, I'll be more than happy to clean it up for you."

"No!" Mathias snapped excitedly before realizing his overzealous tone. "It's an old rug anyway. I'll clean it later."

As Blackstock finished projecting what he believed to be the appropriate amount of empathy, he walked back toward the front door.

"If you need anything, son, just give us a call," he said as he walked back out to his patrol car in the driveway. As he opened the door to the squad, Blackstock looked back and saw Mathias staring at him from the doorway. His expression didn't sit well with Buck, who thought he looked just a little too eager for him to leave, maybe even the hint of a smile.

"Somethin' ain't right with that boy," he mumbled to himself as he drove away down the winding gravel road out of view.

11

As Gideon pulled the Impala into the Fusion Café parking lot, he spied Ryden leaning against his car staring at his watch, beads of sweat forming on his forehead.

"It's about time!" said Ryden.

"Well, what the hell are you standing out here in the heat for? You got air conditioning in the car!"

"You know me. Motor's always running, Sarge!"

Gideon wondered how Jason always stayed so upbeat all the time. Ninety-five degrees outside, in the middle of a nasty homicide investigation, ten hours of sleep in the last week, carrying a load of sixty-plus open cases—and he was still smiling.

"Ya know something, Jason," Gideon said, "sometimes ya just piss me off."

"What'd I do?" Ryden's voice squeaked like a teenager going through puberty.

Gideon smiled, and they walked into the cool confines of the restaurant. The large glass windows fronting Monroe Street allowed plenty of light into the dining area, but the place still felt shadowed and cozy. The awning-covered outdoor decks were empty, mostly, Gideon surmised, because of the heat. A few nondescript patrons milled around inside at various white linen-clad tables. Ryden spotted a twenty-something young man with curly reddish-brown hair standing behind a posh jet-black marble dining counter, cleaning wine glasses. They walked over and took a seat on two red saucer-shaped stools.

"You, Ronnie Shaw?" asked Ryden.

"You must be the cops," he replied, continuing to wipe the rim of the champagne flute.

"You're very astute," Gideon said through clenched teeth.

"I'm guessing then, that the body ya'll found was Lindsay, huh?"

"You don't seem too broken up," Gideon snapped.

Ronnie's face turned pale, even more so than one would expect for a person with red hair and the requisite complexion.

"Listen, she and I dated for a little while, that's all. We split up a few months ago, said she fell out of love with me."

"*Fell out of love?*" Gideon mirrored. He'd been through that one.

"Yeah, you know how women are," said Shaw.

"Oh yeah," said Ryden, looking at Gideon, "all your vast experience in the psyche of the fairer sex and all."

Gideon couldn't help but smile.

My boy! he thought. *He's learning.*

Ronnie leaned back against the counter behind the bar as if defeated. "She was used to having money. Her daddy was a lawyer with bucks, kind of a corporate contract hitman, if you will. Lindsay used to tell me that companies paid him big money to tie up the little people's lawyers in court, saved these businesses millions. He, in turn, got millions, which she had unlimited access to. We were from two different worlds. I grew up upper middle class at best. I wasn't gonna figure into her future plans, and I knew it. She was simply going to be one of those old flames that I brought up on occasion to piss off my future middle-class ex-wife. When I saw on the news that they'd found her car at the park, I got a little spooked."

"Why?" Gideon asked.

"Because I took her there on one of our first dates . . . to look at birds and nature and stuff. One of my professors told me about the place. I thought maybe she'd think I was cultured or something."

"Very sensitive," said Ryden. "Did it work?"

"Did what work?"

"Did it get you in her pants?"

"Fuck you!" Ronnie said, walking toward the other end of the bar. He turned back toward Gideon. "Listen, I know what it sounds like, but for what it's worth, we really did love each other at some point. Was she really mutilated like they said on the news?"

Gideon paused. "Something like that, Ronnie. When was the last time you talked to her?"

"Probably a day or so before you guys found her."

"Did she mention what she was up to? Maybe something about her work at the TV station?" Ryden prodded.

"No, I don't think so. All she mentioned was that she thought her boss was trying to get in her pants, and he threw her some bull-shit assignment about trying to get a human interest story on animals or something. I was the one who suggested that she should do the birds at the park thing."

"Did you go with her?" Gideon asked.

"No, I offered . . . but she said she was gonna show him."

"Show who?" said Ryden.

"Her boss," said Shaw.

"She said a call had come into the station from some guy. Said that he knew someone that had been murdered years ago. Said that the cops knew who did it, but nobody ever went to jail, and he wanted to blow the whistle. He was gonna give her all the gory details, and she was gonna break the story herself. She figured that if she pulled it off, her boss would have no choice but to give her a full-time reporting gig or something."

"This guy have a name?" Gideon asked.

"No," Shaw continued, an addled look washing over him. "Funny thing, now that I think about it, she said that he wouldn't tell her his name over the phone, but he specifically asked for her."

"She told you that?" Ryden asked.

"Wait a minute," said Gideon, "who knew she was working there? She was just an intern, right?"

"Could have been anyone. A few days before, the station had done a feel-good story on itself, letting the community know how much it did to help the local universities. They'd actually introduced all the interns at the end of one of the news broadcasts."

Ryden queried Gideon, "Can't we trace the phone call into the station?"

"Are you insane? Do you have any idea how many calls that station gets in a day? Not to mention the fact that if this is our guy, I doubt very seriously he called from his own phone."

"Yeah, well, there's that," Ryden said dejectedly.

Gideon turned to Ryden, briefly contemplating a smack to the forehead.

"Listen, Ronnie," Gideon said, sliding his card across the bar, "if you think of anything else, call me anytime. I don't sleep."

"He really doesn't," Ryden interjected.

Gideon rolled his eyes, spun around the bar stool and hopped off, making for the door, Ryden in tow. As he opened the door and walked into the parking lot, the mugginess of the evening washed over him like a blanket.

"So now what?" Jason asked.

Gideon stared blankly out onto Monroe Street watching the capital city head home for the night. "We take a break," he said. "Go home, Jason. Kiss your wife and baby girl, and take a break. We'll get on it first thing in the morning."

He hopped into the Impala and limped toward the condo through rush hour traffic. Gideon realized he'd only slept for a couple of hours in the days prior to Eddie waking him up about finding Lindsay. After twenty minutes, he'd traveled the four blocks and pulled into the parking garage. As he entered the elevator, he wondered what Lindsay Diaz had stumbled across, or more appropriately, what had stumbled across her in the twilight of a muggy evening in a desolate, wooded ravine. He slid the key into the lock and pushed open the door to the apartment. Standing there, for a moment, he still expected that maybe she would be sitting there waiting to surprise him. The ghostly figure he envisioned evaporated before him.

This blows, he thought. Closing the door behind him, he walked over to the desk, grabbing the picture of him and Liz from Trey's last Fourth of July party at the lake, with her in a black knit sweater with a white T-shirt underneath. *She was always cold.* He tapped preset number one on the CD player on the floor. Theory of a Deadman's "Santa Monica," chased away the silence as he collapsed on the couch. The streetlights below barely lit the room as he stared at the photograph of the two of them smiling so much in the seemingly distant past. He remembered the first time he'd played the CD on their first trip out of town together to Apalachicola. On the way over the Walker Bridge, she changed the song halfway through. He loved the song because it reminded him of her. He'd played it over and over again often, fighting with a bottle of gin in the interim. Now, he realized he should have seen the sign. His eyes fell heavily closed as the picture fell to his chest. Tomorrow would be another day.

I 2

The baking sunlight beamed through the basswood blinds and blanketed Gideon's face. His eyes still closed, he squinted to keep the unwelcome invader at bay. He rolled and turned himself toward the back of the couch. He felt a coldness on the tip of his nose and opened his eyes to the Fourth of July photograph resting just inches from his face, the glass in the frame pressed against him.

"Fuck me," he grumbled, pulling himself upright. "Can't get her to stay . . . can't get her to go away." He glanced at his watch through puffed, half-open eyes.

"Shit! Nine o'clock!" he squawked.

He dropped his face into his hands, rubbing his eyes to a semblance of coherence; then, looking up, he stared out through the sliding glass doors overlooking downtown.

"Where you at, you piece o' shit?" he mumbled.

Gideon stood and walked over to the kitchen counter, flipping open the phone book to the yellow pages. The only section longer than the attorneys was the escorts. He opened the attorney section to *A* and brushed his finger down the page until he came to Nelson Diaz. He reached into his pocket and fumbled for the cell phone, dialing the number.

"Diaz and Associates," a pleasant woman's voice resonated.

"Yeah," he replied, still fumbling through the drowsiness, "my name is Gideon Kane. I need to set up an appointment with Mr. Diaz."

"Well, sir, Mr. Diaz is out of the office right now. Is this regarding a legal matter?"

Gideon suddenly felt a slight touch of "Are you that fucking stupid?" coming on but checked the thought before he could verbalize it.

"Sort of. I'm the detective assigned to his daughter's murder. You think there's a chance he could squeeze me in today?" he replied, sarcasm spewing from his voice.

"Oh," said the woman, "I'm sorry. Mr. Diaz has an opening at two o'clock. Will that be acceptable?"

"That'll be just splendid," he said. "See you then."

As he hung up the phone, the thought occurred to him: *Who goes to work, scheduling a full day, when their daughter's been brutally murdered less than twenty-four hours ago?*

The unpleasant thought still hung in the air over him when the phone buzzed again.

"Kane," he said.

"Gideon, it's Laura Jernigan. I've got those photos back from the lab. When can you be here?"

"Gimme about an hour or two, Doc," he said. "It's been a rough night, and I need a chance to clear my head."

"Good enough," she said. "There's no Benihana scheduled for today, so I'll be in my office all morning. See you in a few hours, Gideon."

Gideon clicked the phone shut and dropped back down on the couch. Something in Laura's voice was different somehow—somewhere between sultry and scared. He wasn't sure which. Gideon's ADD kicked in, and his eyes scanned over to the liter bottle of gin sitting on the kitchen counter, then back to the picture. His head hurt. The pain behind his eyes felt reminiscently like a hangover headache, but without the prior benefits of the booze. She had that effect on him. Elizabeth hadn't been around in four months. She hadn't even talked to him as a matter of fact—no phone calls, no messages, no nothing. He wondered how they'd gotten to this point.

The brown paper bag from the library caught his eye on the floor beneath the couch. He picked it up, rolled the paper back, and examined the cover: *The Lesser Key of Solomon.*

Gideon realized that Stephanie and the *Kama Sutra* had made him forget all about the fact that he'd pretty much stolen the other book. He opened the cover and began flipping through the pages. The book first appeared in the seventeenth century and was an ancient manuscript purported to be written by King Solomon himself—where details of spirits and the conjurations needed to invoke them were spelled out in great detail, as were the instructions to gain control over them and make them oblige.

What the hell am I doing? he thought. *This is ridiculous.*

As he read on, page after page described, meticulously, the protective signs and rituals to be performed to procure any manner of desires; the names of the seventy-two demons which Solomon was said to have invoked and confined in a brass vessel to do his bidding were shown; and the evocation of all classes of spirits, some good, some evil, some indifferent. And then there were Bune, Bifron, and Murmur—three demons who held dominion over the dead.

Gideon felt a chill as he read the names and glanced up and around the room, scanning all about him. *This is nuts,* he thought. He looked back down and read on about the triumvirate of the dead:

Bune was considered a Great Duke of Hell, commanding thirty legions of demons. Bune was the hellish royalty who commanded the living and the dead.

Bifron commanded six legions and stood charge of changing corpses from their original graves unto other places.

And then there was Murmur. The fifty-fourth spirit of the key. Murmur was also a Great Duke and appeared in the form of a warrior, riding a Gryphon. The three together controlled the immediate afterlife and the time of passing. Murmur took possession of the souls.

"He who speaketh their names may change the place of the dead."

And there it was. Gideon laid the book down on the couch and gazed up and out of the window at the city beneath. He thought about the possibility that it could be that simple, that it could really be just some fucking nutcase who thought he could really bring back the dead. In homicide, nine times out of ten, it wasn't some sinister series of calculated events—it was merely some complete and total loon with a personal agenda, even if that agenda happened to include zombies and ritual sacrifice. He stared out over countless hundreds on the streets below walking aimlessly through their day with absolutely no idea that a lunatic with a God complex might be their next-door neighbor—the man sitting next to them on the bus, the guy standing in front of them at Starbucks, or even the guy teaching their kids algebra.

Gideon reached for the cell phone as he pulled the slip of paper from between the pages of the *Kama Sutra*. Gideon dialed, and the phone rang twice.

"Hello?"

"Uh, hey, Stephanie, this is Detective Gideon Kane," he said. "We met at the library yesterday."

"Oh, how are you? I was hoping you'd call . . . wait a minute, you're a cop?"

"Yeah," he stammered. "Nuts, huh? Listen, the reason I called is about the book."

"Oh, right, sorry about that. I know it was kind of forward and everything."

Gideon realized his lack of clarification.

"No no no . . . not that one," he said, feeling his face flush. "That one was a great surprise, really. Maybe we can get together and talk about it sometime. Actually, I was calling about the other one, the one you let me take without checking it out? Is there any way to tell who's checked this book out before?"

"Absolutely," she said. "The event history of every book in the library is kept on file in the central server in the basement. Detective . . . sorry . . . Gideon, nowadays, you can still buy a ticket and fly on a commercial airline without a driver's license, but you can't get a library card in this city without two forms of valid identification."

"Seriously?" he asked.

"No joke," she answered rather matter-of-factly.

"Do ya think I might be able to get a peek at those records?"

"C'mon, Detective, you know you would need a subpoena to get access to those files."

"Yeah, but—"

She interrupted, her voice teasingly dry, "Unless, of course, you might happen to know somebody . . . Do you know somebody, Detective?"

"Uh, I'm not sure . . . Do I?"

"We close at nine. Come to the side door, off of Bronough Street. I'll meet you there."

"Nine o'clock, got it. Oh, and uh, thanks, Steph, I owe you one."

"Oh, I'd say you owe me a couple," she said, mocking him.

Gideon smiled as he snapped the phone shut. He wasn't exactly sure what he had just accomplished. He *was* sure that he hadn't misread the intimation, but how long was that going to last when she finally realized that he was searching for zombies and demons and such? There was a reason the Dungeons & Dragons crowd never got laid in high school, after all.

The phone buzzed in his hand, and he looked down to see Trey's number.

"Hey, Trey, what's up?"

"Hey, buddy. You're gonna love this. Guess where I'm standing?"

"Gee, Trey . . . I got nothing . . . Where are you standing?"

"I'm standing in the Starbucks on West Tennessee Street."

"Well, that's great, Trey. They make fine cup of coffee. Thanks for sharing."

Trey continued, "While I agree that they do, indeed, make a fine cup o' joe, this particular establishment apparently has some really brilliant clientele."

"Do tell," Gideon said, a note of irritation in his voice.

"Well, it seems that a certain gentleman, who was apparently low on funds, decided that it would be a good idea to walk in the front door with a gun and procure certain assets from the proprietors without their consent."

"Okayyy . . . and?"

"Well, herein lies the rub. This particular gentleman decided to perform this, shall we say, hostile takeover, while a patrol car with two SWAT guys in it was sitting at the drive-through window."

"Ooh," Gideon said, "this is gonna get really stupid in a second, isn't it?"

"Quite." Trey answered. "These guys saw the whole thing go down through the window. They never even got out of their car. Fired twenty-two rounds through the drive-through and didn't miss one shot. This guy's lying here on the floor with more holes in him than a bad nose job. Funny thing is, the SWAT guys said he waved at them as he walked in the door. Darwinism at its finest. Saved the taxpayers the cost of a trial, I guess. Anyway, just called to let you know I'm gonna be tied up on this for a while, so I don't know when I'm gonna be able to help out with the eyeball thing."

"That's fine." Gideon said. "Do me a favor and call Joe Powell over in burglary. See if we can't get him loaned to us until this is over."

"Will do."

Gideon clicked off the phone and fell back onto the couch, rubbing his brow. As his eyes came back into focus, he cocked his head as his gaze fell back on the book. He thought about how ridiculous the whole thing seemed—that he was a grown man, a professional law enforcement officer, and he was sitting here knee-deep in a world of witches and zombies and psychics, not to mention horny librarians. It was going to be impossible to even broach this line of thinking back at the office with any kind of seriousness because deep down, every cop was just an adult who refused to grow up—a childish prankster with a gun. He could already hear the chuckles from each and every one of the guys, and if he was wrong, he would never live it down. There would be the obligatory *Dawn of the Dead* jokes, or somebody would show up to work wearing a witch hat or zombie mask, the watercooler transformed into a bubbling cauldron. He laughed quietly at himself as his shoulders slumped, and he glanced over at the clock—*10:30, and the day already sucked*, he thought.

13

Back out on the streets, young coeds strutted down the sidewalks around downtown in halters and minis and short shorts. As the temperature went up, the amount of clothing diminished proportionately. Summers in Tallahassee were unbearable more often than not, but the heat did bring out some nice scenery on occasion.

As Gideon tooled down the road, his thoughts drew back to Lindsay Diaz. Was she just in the wrong place at the wrong time, or had she been purposefully selected? The amount of damage had indicated some serious planning, so he doubted that it had been random. Ronnie Shaw had said that she was initially going to do a human interest piece on birds at the park, but then there was the mystery phone caller wanting to blow the whistle on the unrequited murder. And why had the caller asked for her? If you really wanted to get something done, wouldn't you want a seasoned reporter instead of an intern? Gideon knew there had to be more to that angle, but he just couldn't put his finger on it yet, and it was pissing him off. Maybe she'd decided to consolidate the two and told the mystery man to meet her there. If he turned out to be full of shit, then she could still do the bird story thing. That is, of course, assuming that he wasn't bringing her there to kill her. If that was the case, then he hadn't called the television station looking for just any reporter. He hadn't been looking for a reporter at all. He'd been looking for Lindsay Diaz. Gideon wondered if it was something she'd done, something she'd seen and shouldn't have. Maybe something she didn't do that she should have. That was a lot of maybes for a twenty-something.

Maybes came with life experience, and according to Ronnie, other than shopping, Lindsay didn't have too many maybes.

Gideon pulled into the parking lot adjacent to the Starbucks. A yellow crime scene tape was strung around the perimeter of the business. Trey was standing just inside the front door talking to one of the SWAT guys, and he ducked under the tape and walked over to him. As he stepped inside, he saw what was left of the bad guy lying on his back next to the counter: his arms and legs splayed about at impossible angles. His eyes and mouth were wide open, and he had a sort of "Holy shit! Where did you guys come from?" look on his face. *Twenty-two rounds of forty-five caliber ammo sure did make a mess,* he thought.

Gideon knelt down and studied the robber's pistol lying on the floor next to his head. He noted that the orange cap on the barrel had been mostly covered up with a black Magic Marker. This was a trick used by most two-bit thieves of today's generation. Almost all water pistols and toy guns had Day-Glo orange caps on the end of the barrel to signify, to anyone wondering, that this gun was indeed a toy. The bad guys, on the other hand, had realized that it was much easier to walk into Walmart and plunk down five dollars on a toy and two dollars on a Sharpie than it was to fill out the paperwork and wait three days for the real thing. Besides, the poor victims were usually too scared to give a shit, and the laws in Florida actually lessened the penalties if the gun wasn't real. *Ya just had to love the Second Amendment,* he thought. Trey finished swapping stories with the SWAT guy and walked over to Gideon.

"Don't you kind of feel sorry for these idiots sometimes?" Gideon said.

"Why?" said Trey. "If they weren't so stupid all of the time, we wouldn't be so brilliant some of the time."

"How long did it take you to come up with that one?" Gideon said, rolling his eyes.

"Just made that one up. Whaddya think?"

"I think you've been hanging around me too much. And now I'm starting to wonder why."

Gideon pressed his hands against his knees and stood up, turning toward Trey, rubbing his brow, and staring back down at the body.

"What kind of fucked up karma do you have to have to bring a toy gun into the one coffee shop in the city that's got two SWAT guys sitting in the drive-through?"

"I dunno . . . *bad* karma?"

Gideon smirked without looking at him. "How much longer you gonna be?" he asked.

"Actually there's not a whole lot left. Just a couple more witness statements, and then, of course, scraping John Dillinger here off the floor. Maybe an hour?"

"Good. Meet me at Nelson Diaz's office at two," said Gideon, handing him a slip of paper with the address.

"Cool. We gonna do the good cop bad cop thing?"

"I was thinking more along the lines of the bad cop . . . bad cop thing. Something isn't right with this whole mess, Trey, and I'm thinking that Nelson Diaz might know more than even *he's* aware of."

"You think it's someone trying to get back at *him* by killing his daughter?"

"I don't know yet," said Gideon. "But something bothers me about the phone call to the TV station before she died. I still can't explain why anyone would specifically ask for the intern rather than an actual reporter. I mean . . . all of us have that one reporter that we trust, that we would confide in about our cases, and that takes years to build up that kind of rapport. So if you've got information on a homicide that the cops apparently didn't give a shit about, why would you trust an intern? It doesn't make any sense."

"Gideon, ya know that I love you, man . . . but would it kill you, just for once, to not think that there's some grand conspiracy behind everything? That maybe it *really* is just some fucking lone nutcase out for a joyride on the homicide highway."

"Yes," Gideon said.

"Yes what?"

"Yes, it would kill me."

"People are gonna start calling you Fox Mulder, ya know that?"

"That's fine. I kinda like Duchovny. Now that you mention it, Scully was kind of hot too . . . oh shit the redhead . . . Jernigan! Trey, I'm late for the morgue. Meet me at Nelson's at two, got it?"

"I'm there, Mulder."

Gideon ran outside, ducking under the crime scene tape and jumped in the car. East on Tennessee Street, he couldn't stop thinking about the phone call. He flipped open the phone and dialed Ryden.

Jason's overly chipper voice resonated, "Hey, Sarge. What's up?"

"Jason, has Joe Powell showed up yet?"

"As a matter of fact, he just walked in about two minutes ago. He's staring at the pile of shit on his desk and speaking in tongues."

"Wonderful. Take him, and get over to channel six. See if anybody remembers any other strange phone calls from this mystery guy, and see if they'll let you check out Lindsay's desk. Look for papers, Post-it notes, anything that might give us an idea as to what she was up to that night."

"You got it, dude," Ryden said glibly.

"I'll be at the morgue if you find out anything."

Gideon flipped the phone shut. *It wasn't Jason's fault,* he thought. But did he *always* have to be in such a damn good mood? Gideon tried to remember the last time that he had been glad to come to work. After a few seconds and limited success, he tried to remember the last time he was happy about anything.

I got nothin' here, he thought.

Gideon made good time to the hospital. He chalked it up to the good ol' media blitz the night before. The news ran a story about how TPD's traffic unit was up in Washington, DC, somewhere competing for the Greatest Ticket Writer Award or some other nonsensical bullshit. TPD loved to have itself in the limelight, and their tall, rather gangly public information officer never missed a chance to let the city know how fortunate they were to have the best damn cops around. Gideon had his share of run-ins with Lurch, as he affectionately referred to him—mainly over who got credit for what. The relationship between the sheriff's office and the police department had always been contentious at best. It really just kind of boiled down to a polyester-clad turf war.

In any event, Lurch's brilliant idea to self-promote the traffic unit essentially just let everyone in Tallahassee know that they had a free pass to speed, blow red lights, and generally have complete and utter disregard for the safety of themselves as well as others. Gideon loved it when TPD imploded, and he smiled.

He zipped into the parking garage and scooted onto the elevator and mashed the floor button the requisite six times. Jernigan's office was right next door to the pathology lab. He'd often thought that at some point it had been a closet because other than Jernigan and her desk, there almost wasn't enough room for a second person. He surmised that ME's didn't have a lot of visitors, for obvious reasons—*mainly the smell*, and their clientele always slept in the other room anyway.

The door opened out, and Gideon spotted Jernigan sitting at her desk, feet propped up, and staring through a magnifying glass at a large photograph.

"Whatcha lookin at?" he asked.

"Oh," she answered, startled, "didn't see you come in."

"I couldn't come in if I wanted to. Is that her?"

"Yeah, this is a blow-up of that mark below the figure eight on her back, but I still can't quite make out what it says. Might be a *Z* or something."

Gideon grabbed the photo and pressed the magnifying glass up to his eye. "Z-E-I-S something," he said almost asking.

He had no idea what it meant, and Jernigan shook her head in agreement. Laura reached over on the desk and handed Gideon a second photo showing the bizarre symbol that had been cut into Lindsay's chest.

"Can I take these?" he asked. "I've got a couple of people that might be able to help."

"They're all yours," she said.

As Gideon placed the photos in an envelope, Laura removed her glasses, laid them on the desk, and glanced up at him.

"I'm going to get another one of these aren't I?" she asked, fearing the inevitable answer.

"I hope not."

She stood up and brushed her right hand across Gideon's arm. "Catch him."

"I'm trying," he whispered as he walked away down the hall.

As he stood alone in the elevator, the old refrain replayed itself: *If Gideon doesn't catch 'em, no one will!*

He glanced at his watch and realized he still had an hour before the meeting with Diaz. He hopped off the elevator and made his way to the parking garage, jumping into the Impala. He'd decided that if anyone might be able to make sense of this, it would be Lillian Langdale. He pointed the car toward East Tennessee Street—and blew the light.

14

Mathias watched from the front door as the deputy backed out of the driveway and slowly pulled away, disappearing around the first bend of the gravel road. He turned back toward the hallway and stared at the spot on the rug.

Mud . . . the dumb son of a bitch thought it was mud! The voice in his head taunted him.

Mathias turned quickly and ran through the house, out the back door, past the shed, and onto the path through the woods. His mind racing, he tripped once on the path that he'd traveled hundreds of times, skinning his knee. He lay motionless on the ground for a moment, staring up through the trees at the sky, thoughts of Mother assaulting his consciousness. He sat up and stared at the tear in his jeans as he watched the blood soak into the fabric. *Strange*, he thought, *there was no pain.* After a moment, he stood again and scrambled down the remaining forty yards of woods onto the river bank. He looked north, up toward the direction of the bridge, and saw the plume of smoke in the distance sprinting down the edge of the wood line. After several minutes, he'd reached an outcropping below where the bridge had once been. A mound of fresh timber lay at the base in all directions. Mathias hunched down behind a cypress stump and watched as troopers scurried about like ants over the pile, trying to locate Mother's car beneath the deluge. The single red flashing light from the ambulance to the north cast an intermittent crimson glow over the scene as day turned to dusk. He watched as Deputy Blackstock pulled his cruiser up to the south side of the bridge and ambled his way down the embankment to where the remains of where Mother's car was believed to be. He could hear the troopers on the north side talking about the truck driver and how he'd been in a hurry and shouldn't have been driving on the narrow gravel road in the first place. He overheard them say that the load hadn't been secured properly and that he most certainly was speeding, that the truck driver was uninjured, and that the most they could do to him was issue him a citation.

His gaze turned back toward the deputy who had managed to wind his way through the maze of fallen logs into a nook at the southwest base of the bridge.

"I've got it!" he yelled to the troopers. "I can see it."

The two troopers who had previously been discussing their lack of ability to do anything scrambled over to where Blackstock was now lying on his stomach, wedged between two crossed timbers. The whole pile looked as if it were about to shift, and Mathias remembered thinking it odd that a man would commit so selflessly for a total stranger. As the troopers reached the wreckage, he watched as they grabbed Blackstock by the belt and lowered him down through the narrow opening into what remained of the car's passenger compartment.

"She's not here!" the deputy yelled.

"Whaddya mean she's not there?" responded the trooper.

"Just what I God damn well said. She ain't in there! Now if you two don't mind getting your heads outta your asses, would anybody mind pulling me the fuck outta here please!"

Mathias spun quickly around and sat against the stump. She's not there, he thought. Maybe she got out before the bridge collapsed. Maybe she had been thrown from the car or maybe even jumped before the logs came crashing down. Maybe she had managed to swim out after the accident and was lying on the shore waiting to be rescued. The maybes kept coming, assaulting his brain to the point of overload. Mathias stood up, took one more momentary glance back toward the bridge, and walked sullenly back the way he had come.

As he made his way, the voice continued to mock him.

It's your fault she's gone!

"No it's not!"

If you had been able to control yourself last night, that girl would still be alive!

"What has that got to do with Mother?" Mathias screamed.

If you hadn't killed that poor girl, Mother would not have gone into town. She would not have had to leave this place!

"What gives you the right?"

Child . . . you pay me far too little confidence. Belial gives me the right . . . Bune gives me the ability . . . and you, dear child . . . give me the capacity! You would do well to pay heed to my words!

"Who is Bune?"

He who speaketh his name may change the places of the dead.

"What in hell does that mean?"

In hell, child . . . it means everything . . .

"Who are you? And what do you want with me?"

I am called Murmur . . . and soon enough, child, you shall know me.

Mathias reached the edge of the footpath where he had sent the Finch girl to her final rest and collapsed on the wet sand. Staring out across the river, he noticed that the current was unusually slow, and the setting sun cast an eerie pall across the glassy surface. *Mother would want me to go on,* he thought to himself. Following the thought, he noticed there was no smart-ass comment from the voice. He pulled his feet up and wrapped his arms around his legs, his head resting on his knees. The water lapped up against the partially submerged stump to his left in frequent intervals, and he took in the peaceful sounds of the slow-moving water. Then suddenly, the sound gave way to silence. It took him a moment to realize that the sound had changed, and he looked up, gazing to his left at the stump, the setting sun reflecting a glint off of something at the outer base of the log. He stood up slowly, brushed the sand from his trousers, and walked slowly toward the flash. Reaching the log, he knelt down as the hand bobbed to the surface, and he fell backward catching himself—a solitary emerald ring on the middle finger. She hadn't left him after all.

12

Joe Powell was a good burglary cop. Gideon had asked for him over the others available for several reasons. Number one of which was that he was tenacious, and that was a good trait for a homicide cop. The second was that he was smarter than most. Powell was a large man, intimidating to most. He was not so much tall but just plain big. The kind of big that made people think twice about lying, else face the retribution that he just seemingly projected. On the inside, he was just a big pussycat, but few got to know that side of him since, like Gideon, he didn't much associate with too many people beyond other cops and the people he was sending away. The third reason, well, he was just kind of fun to be around. He was, for lack of a better term, a country bumpkin. Not so much the bumpkin, but more of the country. A corn-fed southern boy who didn't take kindly to bad guys taking advantage of the weak, and a huge fan of good ol' southern fried cooking or any cooking for that matter.

Looking over at Ryden, Powell asked, "Can we stop and grab something to eat?"

"Dude, this ain't burglary. You in homicide now. We ain't got time to eat. You know, the whole first forty-eight hours thing?" Ryden's best fake country accent was failing.

"If you don't pull through a drive-through, there's *gonna* be a homicide, rook."

The television station was on Thomasville Road, and as Ryden pulled off Monroe Street, he spied the solution to his right.

"How about a double Whataburger with cheese? Will that work for ya?"

"It'll keep Gideon from having another case to work," said Powell.

Ryden slowed and pointed the car toward the parking lot and into the drive-through to avoid what he correctly anticipated as imminent pain.

A number one with cheese and a large diet soda later . . .

"Do you have any idea what that thing you're shoveling into your mouth is doing to your body?" Ryden asked.

"I don't give a shit. My body says it's time for dead animal flesh, and I must obey," said Powell as a fistful of fries disappeared behind pearly whites. "Kinda like when your wife asks you if it's okay if you spend the weekend visiting with her parents. You just know that it's gonna be bad for you, but then you come to the sensible conclusion that the short-term benefits greatly outweigh any long-term cardio-vascular liability."

"There's something seriously wrong with you, man."

"Why do you have to give me shit because I'm in touch with my inner carnivore?"

Ryden smiled as he turned into the parking lot of the television station.

"Just do me a favor, finish chewing, and for God's sake, wipe the ketchup off your shirt before we go inside."

"Ya know," said Powell, "you're very shallow. There's too much obsession with appearances nowadays, and you skinny fuckers are the reason this country's going to shit."

"Oh, just get outta the car."

"Go ahead and start without me. Ya know us fat fucks need a little extra time!"

"Oh, now you're just being ridiculous."

"Ichabod Crane!" barked Powell.

"Orca!"

The two of them stood in the parking lot for the next several minutes tossing barbs at each other across the roof of the car like two schoolchildren before the security guard came sauntering over.

"Is there a problem, gentlemen?" he asked.

Both of them turned, silent, and froze their gaze.

As the guard raised his hands and turned back away from them, they turned back toward each other.

"Ya know something, rook," Powell said, "you're all right. Now whaddya say we go inside and make somebody squeal like Ned Beatty in *Deliverance*."

Jason yielded, a faint smile forming on his face.

"Ya know something, Powell, this could be the start of a beautiful friendship."

They walked inside the lobby and made their way to the front desk, a pleasant-looking blonde not a day over twenty tossed them an empty smile.

"Can I help you, gentlemen?" she asked.

"Yes, ma'am," Powell cut in. "We're here to see Hank McNamara."

"Do you have an appointment?"

"Well, no, ma'am, but we're with the sheriff's office and if you—"

"Mr. McNamara is very busy, and if you don't have an appointment, I'm afraid that seeing him will be impossible."

Powell's face flushed, and he looked over at Ryden rolling his eyes toward the girl. *Well . . . work it, pretty boy.*

Jason took his cue, eyeing the receptionist's bronze-colored plastic nameplate. "Listen . . . Tiffany, I know that he's a busy man, but this is about Lindsay Diaz, and if you could just get us a few minutes with Mr. McNamara, I promise that you would be doing me a great personal favor."

Ryden leaned into her and whispered, "My boss here is kind of an asshole, and if we don't get to talk to your boss, then my boss is gonna make my life a living hell."

Mirroring him, she leaned in smiling and twirling her hair. "Let me see what I can do."

Tiffany stood up, her eyes locked to Ryden's as she disappeared through the doorway behind her.

"See what an occasional sit-up and a salad will get ya?" Ryden quipped.

Powell's face flushed again as he turned toward Jason, fist clenched, as Tiffany reappeared.

"Mr. McNamara will see you now," she said, still smiling at Ryden.

Jonathan Henry McNamara was the news director and anchored the six o'clock news broadcast. In a town where it seemed that everyone went by their middle name, Hank did not disappoint. Tall and broad across the shoulders, McNamara was the epitome of the modern anchorman. Perfect teeth announced themselves through a perpetually contrived smile, while his glistening Ken doll hair sat orderly and frozen in place under an Aqua Net glaze. In his late forties, he appealed to the modern soccer moms trapped in lives of hopeless repetition and marriages of convenience. To the twenty-somethings, he reminded them of their childhood and their father's best friend whom they'd always had kind of an innocent crush on since they were old enough to think of such things. And to the sixty and over crowd, well, he was what they had envisioned their now aging spouses to have looked like once upon a lifetime ago.

Hank stood up from behind an immense mahogany desk, spurious smile beaming, as he extended his hand toward the two.

"Detectives," he said, pomposity overflowing, "whatever we here at channel six can do to aid the authorities is not only our pleasure, but our civic responsibility."

Powell felt his face warm as Ryden noticed and glanced down to see his fingers clench.

"You really need to do something about that blood pressure thing," Ryden said, turning back to McNamara.

"Mr. McNamara, we're here about—"

"Lindsay Diaz," Hank interjected, "an amazing girl. So much . . . what's the word I'm looking for?"

"Cleavage?" Powell said sternly.

"Huh? No . . . potential. Yes that's it, potential. Such a pity."

Powell leaned in again. "Why? Cause you didn't get a chance to—"

Ryden, sensing disaster, interrupted, "I think that what my partner was going to say was that you didn't get a chance to see her in action . . . err, no . . . umm, see how good of a reporter she could have been."

"Reporter?" McNamara chuckled. "Gentlemen, she could no more have been a reporter than say . . . you, perhaps."

Powell clenched, and Jason's head dropped as he raised his hand onto Powell's shoulder, holding him in check. Ryden's mind raced, looking for a way out.

"What exactly does that mean, Hank? What was she doing here then?"

"Gentlemen, listen. With three colleges in this town, we have hundreds of college students apply for internships here every year. Maybe one or two have what it takes to make it in this business. The rest are simply disillusioned Hollywood wannabes who figure that this is their ticket to getting on television and being discovered. The fact of the matter is that reciting lines in a movie script is one thing, but being able to convey coherent thought in a logical progression that can be understood and considered interesting by viewers with an eighth grade education, as well as those with a PhD, is quite another. Lindsay was a beautiful girl, but she wasn't prime time material. She was more of a fluffer."

"What the hell is a fluffer?" Powell demanded.

Jason jumped in, "So she was more of an eye candy thing than anyone you were gonna develop, right?"

"Exactly," said Hank. "She was never going to be a feature reporter, but she was pleasing on the eyes, so I gave her the opportunity to do a meaningless human interest piece. Something that she could throw on her resume, but it would never have made it on the show."

"Geez," said Powell, "you're quite the fuckin' saint, huh?"

Ryden burst in, "What was wrong with her, Hank? Why wasn't she gonna make it?"

"She wouldn't play the game!" hollered McNamara.

Powell turned to Ryden, saying, "See . . . I told ya he was a fuckin' saint."

"I have no illusions as to what my job is here, gentlemen. Frankly, all I do is cull the wheat from the chaff, and Lindsay was chaff. It takes more than a pretty face, and I was simply giving her the chance to build some experience."

"What about phone calls?" Ryden asked. "Did she get any strange phone calls?"

"Funny you should mention that. Tiffany said that three or four days before Lindsay . . . passed . . . she started getting phone calls from the same person. Sometimes four and five a day."

"How did she know it was the same person?" said Powell.

"Well, he never told her his name, but she said that he had a really distinct kind of voice. She said that when he called, if Lindsay wasn't available, he would seem to get really angry, and that he would begin to stutter."

"Did he leave a callback number?" Ryden asked.

"No . . . he would just calm down again, and say that he would try back later."

"Did you know where Lindsay was going the night that she died?"

"No, I told her to do the piece on animals . . . because everyone loves animals, but she never mentioned anything in particular. I just assumed she was at the park for the birds."

"Birds?" said Powell.

"Yes. Henry Park is renowned for bird-watching. Hell, that's the only reason people go there. As parks go, it's otherwise pretty vanilla. Didn't you know that?"

"Sure we did," said Ryden, Powell nodding his assent.

"Did she have a workstation?" Ryden added. "Can we take a look?"

"Actually, we've already boxed up her things. Let me get Tiffany to get those for you."

McNamara pushed the intercom, talked down to Tiffany for a moment, and then sat back in his chair, that plastic smile beaming all the while. Powell felt himself losing it, yet all three sat there, silent, for the next few minutes just staring at each other.

Tiffany entered the room and laid the box on the desk in front of Ryden before retreating back to the lobby, staring at Jason as she exited with a devious grin.

Ryden stood and looked over the contents: pens, pencils, the June issue of *Cosmo* detailing one hundred ways to keep him coming back for more—and a single Post-it note.

> *M –*
> *8:00 Henry Park*
> *at the ravine*
> *-bring your glasses!!*

Ryden slipped the note into his pocket and motioned for Powell to stand.

"Mr. McNamara, we appreciate your candor. If you hear of anything else that might help us, please give us a call," Ryden said calmly.

"Yeah," snapped Powell, "it being your fucking civic duty and all."

As they made their way back to the parking lot and approached the car, Powell stopped.

"What?" Jason asked.

"Ya know, Gideon would have let me kick that guy's ass."

16

Gideon closed his eyes and swung open the heavy oak door as he walked into Lillian's place. The trick worked for a moment, but then returned to dark as pitch, with little flecks of starlight from the candles arranged around the room. He felt his way toward the back room and pulled aside the curtain as he spied Lillian sitting at the table with the newspaper.

"What are you doing?" he asked.

She sat staring at the paper, the pencil lead tapping intently against the table.

"Crossword puzzle," she muttered. "I need six letter word for medium. Starts with *O*."

"You're kidding right?"

"No, I am not kidding. What are you doing back here so soon? Two visits in a week, soon you will make me think you have feelings for me," she said smiling. "Sit down, Gideon, I shall put on some tea."

Lillian stood and ambled over to the stove, grabbed the kettle, and filled it with water. Gideon took a seat at the table and laid the envelope in front of him.

"Lillian, I need you to look at some pictures for me, and they're not going to be pretty."

"The case with the eyes," she said, still tending to the kettle.

"Yes," Gideon said dejectedly.

Lillian turned from the stove holding two Crown Staffordshire porcelain teacups. She reserved the good china for special guests, and

Gideon appreciated it. The gold rims gave a slightly metallic taste to the Earl Grey which he found made it less bitter and more palatable. Gideon was a black coffee kind of guy, but Lillian felt that a good cup of tea made everything better. Placing them on the table, she placed her hand over the envelope and slid it toward her.

"Gideon, I know this is what you do, and there is a place for it, but I feel bad things coming from this . . . people close to you. I sense you are dabbling in things that you cannot fight against . . . cannot control."

"And we all know how much of a control freak I am," he said glibly.

Lillian opened the envelope and slid the photographs out and in front of her and gasped briefly, though she did her best to hide it, and Gideon was not about to point it out. She then laid each photo out side by side, tucked her elbows in under her, and leaned over them bobbing back and forth saying nothing. Gideon swore she was humming, but in this building, it could have been any manner of things.

"Oracle," Gideon said matter-of-factly.

Lillian looked up from the table, momentarily, at Gideon with the expression of someone who had just swallowed something sour.

"The six-letter word for medium . . . in the puzzle?" he said.

Her expression then changed to that of someone who had just been given directions in Chinese, and she lowered her gaze back down to the photographs without saying a word.

Lillian raised the picture of the strange carvings on Lindsay's chest up to the candlelight, her finger tapping against the symbol. "This . . . I've seen this one before. But where?" she said, biting her lower lip, frustrated that the answer was nipping at the tip of her tongue.

She stood slowly, mumbling to herself, and turned back toward the kitchen, disappearing through the doorway beyond. Gideon could still hear her talking to herself, and although he desperately wanted to know what she was up to, he knew that he didn't dare interrupt. After several minutes, Lillian returned carrying a rather thick and large brown leather-bound book, its cover easily observed as battered and worn with age.

"What the hell is that?" asked Gideon. "Dracula's phone book?"

"You should mind your tongue, young man."

"Sorry, just tryin' to lessen the creepiness a tad, that's all."

"This is a grimoire, an ancient textbook of magic," she said sternly.

"Oh, come on, Lillian, not again with this shit! Are we really back to all the witch stuff and spells and demons and all that crap?"

Lillian snapped back, "Crap? Yes, we are back to the crap, as you so eloquently put it. What you need to understand, Gideon, is that it does not matter what is real and what is imagined. Perception *is* reality. What people believe doesn't have to be tangible to you . . . it just has to be tangible to them. Just because you don't believe in evil—"

"Oh, I believe in evil," he interrupted.

"Just because you don't believe in *demons* . . . doesn't mean that others don't. And even if they don't actually exist, the belief that they do is a more powerful influence on humanity than you could ever imagine."

"All right, I get the point," he said. "If someone actually believes that their talking to dead people, whether they are or not, then their actions are driven by that delusion. Does that about sum it up?"

Clearly frustrated, she replied, "In an anal-retentive policeman, I-won't-open-my-eyes-to-anything-new sort of way . . . yes."

A slow smile evolved on both of their faces as Lillian laid the grimoire on the table, the dust flying up indicating that she had not touched the book in quite some time.

"So what is this particular book?" Gideon asked.

"This is the Grand Grimoire, *Pseudomonarchia Daemonum*."

"My latin's a little rusty," he said. "Help me out here."

"This is the book which allows you to make contact with the demons of hell. The soldiers of Satan's army," she said, her thick Slavic accent rolling off her tongue.

"Ya know, you're actually not gonna believe this, but I actually went to the library and read something called *The Lesser Key of Solomon*. Ever heard of it?"

Lillian's face turned to disappointment. "This would be that book," she said, "but not some *library* version. Can't you indulge an old woman, just once in a while, her grand entrance? You men are all the same. You don't pay attention, and then when you do, you suck the life energy out of us and wonder why we don't respond to you. You know that's what you did to Elizabeth."

"Oh, for cryin' out loud! You gotta bring that up now?"

"Yes"

"Why?"

"Because you're a man . . . and therefore you deserve it."

Again, the smiles emerged, and they both laughed for a moment. Lillian opened the book and proceeded to explain to Gideon how the symbols carved on Lindsay's chest seemed eerily similar to the Seal of Murmur, the demon in charge of collecting the souls of the dead. As Lillian showed him a picture of the seal, his stomach grew queasy.

Desperately, Gideon posed the question, "So you're telling me that I've got a nutbag out there who honestly thinks that he's speaking to the head demon in charge of soul collecting?"

"Pretty much," she said. "Now drink your tea and have a biscuit. You can't go hunting demons on an empty stomach."

Gideon grabbed a biscuit, and the two of them sat for a while longer talking about demons and dead people—and Elizabeth. Gideon's pocket buzzed, and as he opened the phone, he saw Trey's number.

"Hey, Trey, what's up?"

"What's up? It's almost two. Where the hell are you? I'm sitting in Diaz's waiting room, and I don't mind telling you that it's pretty much a shrine unto himself."

"What does that mean?" Gideon asked.

"Dude's got more paintings of himself in here than Donald Trump. It's kinda creepy. Sorta like the lobby of the Haunted Mansion at Disney World. Ya know the one where the ceiling rises up and the walls stretch? Anyway . . . get down here already. I don't like being the only one in the building without a four-thousand-dollar suit."

"Okay, I'm leaving Lillian's now."

"The psychic?" Trey said. "What the hell are you doing at a psychic?"

"I'll tell ya later."

Gideon finished his tea, stuffed the photos back in the envelope, and thanked Lillian for the biscuits. As he opened the front door, he looked back at her and asked again.

"Whaddya think, Lillian . . . any chance at fixin' this, with *her* I mean?"

Lillian smiled. "As long as there is hope . . . well . . . then there is hope."

God why does she do this shit to me? Gideon thought, shaking his head. *Can't she just answer a simple question? I mean it's not like I'm asking for the lottery numbers or something.*

Gideon jumped in the car and pointed west onto Mahan Drive. *Nelson Diaz . . . you got some splainin' to do . . .*

17

Gideon eased up to the intersection of Magnolia Drive and picked up the cell phone from the console, punching in the numbers. Two rings later—"*Pierce law office . . .*"

His mouth was dry, and as hard as he tried to sound nonchalant, he knew she'd see right through it as soon as he tried to eke out the words.

"Hey, Liz . . ."

"Gideon? How are you?" she said with what he interpreted as a pleasant surprise kind of tone.

"I'm good," he said, quickly coming to terms with the fact that almost undoubtedly he was wrong—again.

"How have you been?" he asked.

"Well, you know . . . okay, I guess all I do is work . . . you?"

"I'm just great . . . I'm good . . . managing . . . umm anyway, listen, I'm actually calling about a case."

"Really? Whaddya got?" she said, curious.

"Well, what do you know about Nelson Diaz?"

Elizabeth hesitated. "Kind of an asshole. Good attorney though . . . if you're looking for that sort of thing, that is."

"What sort of thing would that be?" he asked.

"Well, if you had a shitload of money, and you were guilty as hell, and you needed a lawyer who had enough juice to get you off in a civil case . . . he would be the guy."

"Okay, so by 'shitload,' are we talking Johnny Cochran, O. J. kind of money, or what? I'm guessing that if I just won Jeopardy, I probably still don't have enough to hire him?" Gideon asked.

"No Gideon . . . you're not getting me here. It's more of the other way around," she said. "*You* don't retain *him*. He decides whether you're worthy of his services, and if so, then he *allows* you to hire him. It would be a rather nice problem to have, actually. Why, what's up with him?"

"His daughter was found murdered yesterday, thinking there might be a link to him or his business, somehow."

"Exciting . . . how'd she die?"

"You don't wanna know, trust me."

"Telllll meee!"

Gideon recited quickly and wryly, "Well, her face was caved in, her mouth was sewn shut, let's see . . . she broke her back, strange symbols were carved in her chest . . . and, oh yeah . . . her eyes were removed and are currently unaccounted for. Yeah, that should about cover it."

"Alrighty then," she said. "Good times . . . I should let you go."

"You already did that."

"Cute," she said sarcastically.

"Hey listen, do you wanna maybe grab some dinner later or maybe a drink?"

"I would, Gideon, but I'm gonna be working late in the office, and then I'm taking my ass to the house and curl up in bed with the dogs."

The two matching Westies were always Elizabeth's pride and joy.

"How are Max and Oscar?"

"They're good . . . well, Max is good . . . and you know Oscar. I think they miss you sometimes."

"Great, glad to see someone does."

"Cut it out, Gideon. You know the whole thing wasn't exactly easy for me either. I need some time to figure myself out, okay? So just cut me some slack."

"Slack . . . got it. Hey, how 'bout lunch sometime?"

"I could probably do lunch. Call me."

"Great," he said. "I'll give you a call this week."

As he clicked the phone shut, Gideon pondered whether what had just occurred was progress or not. More than anything, he missed simply talking to her—the everyday banter about nothing in particular, or just hearing her voice.

Gideon arrived at the office of Nelson Diaz and pulled off of East Park Avenue into the driveway running alongside the building. This section of town consisted mainly of somewhat grand Colonial Revival style homes lining narrow residential streets that had long since been converted by the local real estate constituency into prime commercial properties for well-to-do businesses.

Gideon traversed the red brick walkway as it clacked under his feet, and he made his way up to the wide white, oak door centered on the front terrace. Well-worn red and black brick fronted the exterior. He noted the smooth, circular white pillars lining the entryway and thought to himself that this place oddly reminded him of a smaller version of the library. As he grabbed the handle and stepped inside the vestibule, he spied Trey sitting in a Bergere caned-back mahogany chair looking extremely uncomfortable.

"About time you got here," said Trey. "This may be the most expensive uncomfortable chair I've ever sat in. My back's killing me."

"Sorry, I was talking to Liz ,and I got distracted."

"Really? How'd that work out for ya?" An impish grin fully formed.

"I don't have a fuckin' clue, man. She was my best friend for all that time, and all of a sudden I can't read her at all, *but*, on a lighter note, Lillian read my tarot cards, and said that my romantic life was magnetic today . . . that's good, right?"

"Yeah, I guess, but don't magnets attract *and* repel?"

"Well, there's that," Gideon said sullenly. "Why do you always have to bring so much goddamn sunshine to my parade, Trey?"

"That's my job, buddy. Besides, the more screwed up your existence is, the less painful mine seems."

"Thanks."

"Listen, man, I've been telling you to move on for a while, but I understand what you're going through. And as much as I hate to say it, I hope she comes back too. It just wasn't the right time . . . that's all. She was part of the family . . ."—Trey paused and then attempted his best Marlon Brando—"And once you become part of the family, you can never leave."

They both began to laugh as a smallish bespectacled woman appeared from behind the elevated front desk and walked over to them as they continued to toss about the many ways that Gideon had fucked up his marriage and how there was still the distinct possibility that at least some of it wasn't all his fault.

"Mr. Diaz will see you now," she said, motioning them to an adjacent room as she moved ahead of them.

Gideon noticed that Trey had been right. Diaz's office did look more like a pretentious shrine unto himself than a sophisticated place of business. As they walked down the short hallway, Gideon saw yet more tributes in oil lining both walls and wondered when Diaz might have had time to practice law when it seemed that all he did was pose for self-portraits.

Gideon looked over at Trey as they each walked a few steps behind the matronly assistant who didn't seem to be paying them any attention.

"Ya know something?" Gideon said.

"What's that?"

Gideon smiled. "I don't tell you that I love you enough anymore, do I?"

"Ya know, you really don't, and I've been meaning to say something to you about it . . ." Trey spoke a little louder, "we just don't cuddle enough anymore, Gideon."

They both stopped abruptly as they glanced over and realized that the woman had also stopped and looked completely aghast at their repartee.

"Gentlemen," she said, shaking her head and clearing her throat, "through here please."

As they stepped through the doorway, they both laughed and patted each other on the back.

"After you, Mr. Kane."

"No I insist, after you, Mr. Morris."

"Gentlemen, please!" the woman moaned, pleading for them to stop.

Realizing it was time to let her off the hook, they simply smiled some more and walked into the office as she closed the door behind them. As old-school cops, they often felt it their civic duty to make the mostly privileged and pompous rich folk feel as uncomfortable as possible whenever they got the chance. Their work here was done.

Nelson Diaz sat behind a large dark cherry wood desk footed with lion heads at the base of each corner. He was talking on the phone, and Gideon surmised that from the tone of the conversation, things didn't appear to be going Diaz's way. And judging by what Liz had told him, he anticipated that things were going to end badly. After a moment, Diaz explained to the unfortunate soul on the other end of the line, in no uncertain terms, that if things weren't corrected swiftly, whatever those *things* were Gideon could only guess, there would be hell to pay. At that point, Diaz quickly slammed down the phone, his previously noxious grin giving way to a pathetic imitation smile as he stood and extended his hand toward Gideon.

"Nelson Diaz, gentlemen,"—now motioning them to have a seat—"What can I do for you?"

"Mr. Diaz, I'm Sergeant Kane. This is Detective Morris. We're investigating your daughter's murder."

Diaz sat back in his chair, closed his eyes, and pinched the bridge of his nose between two fingers. Gideon thought he'd seen a tear form, but he wasn't sure. He liked to know a little bit about his suspects before he interviewed them. He felt it gave him a direction to take the conversation, and leading the conversation in the desired direction was textbook interview practice. Elizabeth had given him a little background, albeit from a personal bias, and he didn't want to lock himself into a particular opinion at this point. Diaz, however, was not a suspect, but something about him bothered Gideon. He just didn't seem upset enough, and something still annoyed him about the fact the Diaz was actually in his office while his daughter was still on the slab at the morgue.

Diaz sat forward. "Detective Kane . . . Lindsay was my only child. If there is anything that I can do to aid you in your investigation, please do not hesitate to ask."

"Do you know who killed her?" Gideon asked abruptly.

Trey squirmed in his seat as he turned toward Gideon with an almost identical look of shock that Diaz immediately displayed.

"Excuse me?" Diaz replied, standing quickly from his chair.

Trey also stood, finally realizing that Gideon had begun a frontal assault.

Turning toward Gideon, Trey said, "Ohhh, we're going that route . . . good play."

Deliberately now, Gideon asked, "Mr. Diaz, do you know anything about the death of your daughter?"

"Detective Kane, if you're insinuating that I had anything to do with what that goddamn monster did to my little girl . . . then you are as insane as he!"

"Listen, Mr. Diaz, I'm not *insinuating* anything. It's just that your daughter was a twenty-two-year-old college student. A communications major aspiring to be the next Katie Couric, like thousands before her. And as cold as this sounds, I realize that she was your baby girl and, therefore, special to you in a way that no one else could be. But the fact of the matter is . . . she wasn't . . . special, I mean. By all accounts, not special enough for someone to do the things to her that they did. That means only one of two things . . . that she knew something she shouldn't have . . . or someone close to her did."

As Diaz collapsed back down into his chair, face in hands, Trey did the same, looking back at Gideon, smiling and performing a silent golf clap.

"Mr. Kane, don't you think that if I had any clue as to who might have done this to Lindsay . . . that I would tell you?"

"I know you would, sir," Gideon replied trying to sound like someone who was being condescending but pretending not to be.

"But perhaps you don't realize that you might know something . . . maybe something about *the way* she died. Is there anything in your past, maybe an old client that you lost a case for—"

"*I don't lose, Mr. Kane!*" Diaz protested.

Gideon sat silent, locking his gaze, which had now returned to the aforementioned noxious variety.

Trey interjected, still smiling, "Alrighty then. Mr. Diaz, I think what Sergeant Kane is trying to say here is that maybe you're just not *aware* that you have said knowledge that might actually be helpful to us, and not that you would *ever* be intentionally holding anything back."

Gideon and Diaz continued to survey one another, all but ignoring him.

Trey slowly, "Coz that would be absurd . . . right, Gideon?"

"Is that what you're trying to say, Detective Kane?" Diaz posed through clenched teeth.

Gideon paused then said, "Mr. Diaz, I am trying to catch your daughter's killer, that's all. What happened to her took a lot of rage . . . and a lot of planning. Lindsay's life experience just doesn't add up to that kind of final act. I think there's a distinct possibility that someone may have been trying to get back at you through her."

Diaz's face contorted as he listened, and Gideon thought he might actually be getting through to the narcissistic bastard.

"Detective, I assure you that if I knew *anything*, I would tell you. Now, as it seems that we have established that I am not aware of any mitigating factors in the death of my daughter, any further discussion would simply be a waste of your time, and thus just further preempt you from catching this sick son of a bitch. Therefore, I won't take up any more of your time. Good day, gentlemen. Mona will see you out."

Trey and Gideon stood as Gideon tossed his card on the desk.

"If you *do* think of anything, Mr. Diaz," Gideon said, "please call me. I don't sleep much."

With that, Trey and Gideon turned and walked back through the door past Mona who was motioning them back toward the lobby.

"Neither do I, Mr. Kane," Nelson whispered, "neither do I."

As Trey walked back past Mona's desk, he snagged a Ghirardelli chocolate from the porcelain chafing dish and followed Gideon outside onto the front entryway.

Trey popped the chocolate into his mouth, and pointing his thumb back over his shoulder, said, "That guy's a *dick*, ya know that? I mean, I've seen dicks . . . and that's a *huge* one. And I'm not talkin' girth here either,"—spreading his hands apart—"I'm talkin' like serious length on this one . . . and not in a good way, I mean."

Gideon looked up, brow furrowed. "Thank you, Trey. Appreciate the explicit commentary."

"Anything I can do to help. You mind if I go back in and get another one of those chocolate thingies? 'Cause that was really tasty."

Gideon shook his head and began walking back toward the driveway as Trey followed.

"What?" Trey said as he walked. "That was a truly exceptional chocolate. You don't get that kind of stuff down here at the municipal pay scale. Ya know, Gideon, you need to learn to appreciate the finer things that life has to offer."

Gideon's head throbbed.

Back inside, Nelson Diaz sat in a semi-fetal position in his burgundy leather chair.

"Nelson," Mona said, "can I do something for you?"

Without looking up, he said, "Get Sam Tate on the phone . . . from SJP Trucking. Tell him that we might . . . scratch that . . . *he* might have a problem."

18

Mathias sat motionless in the sand, fixated on the emerald ring as it gently bobbed side to side with the current. After a moment, he noticed that there was no sound, save his own heart beating restlessly out of his chest. He noticed that the nail on the ring finger had been broken, and he caught himself thinking how Mother had always taken such pride in her appearance and how upset she would be that her nails were no longer perfectly manicured.

"I'm sorry, Mother," he whispered, "I shall fix things, I promise."

Mathias rocked to his knees and began to crawl slowly toward her.

Careful, young one, the voice echoed.

Mathias quickly snapped back, recoiling against the log and scanning the forest line.

"Where are you?" he yelled. "Show yourself!"

In due time, child, in due time . . . You have much work to do, and there is little time for idle chat.

Mathias turned his head, looking back down at Mother. "What work? What am I to do?"

It will not take those policemen long to discover she is here. You must work quickly to prepare her for the return.

"Return? What return?"

For the next several moments, Mathias carried on a heated dialogue with the voice, as if there was someone standing there with him on the bank. A passerby would most certainly have thought him mad as he stood animated, arguing with himself. After another moment, Mathias turned and walked over and knelt down beside her. He grabbed the hand, shrinking back at first, before taking hold a second time and pulling her onto the bank. He sat down next to her, her head cradled in his lap and his arms enveloping her. His eyes closed, he took a moment to remember the way she had been. As his eyes opened again, he looked down at her and, for the first time, saw the anguish on her twisted face. Her eyes were open, and she looked up at him with what Mathias had realized must have been the same expression she carried as life escaped her.

You know what you must do, young one. Quickly . . . remove the essence, and protect it always for the coming.

Mathias paused for a moment, staring into her distant eyes as a tear welled in his own. He dug his right hand into his pocket and fumbled around before removing an old Case red bone sheep's-foot pocketknife.

"I'm so sorry, Mother . . ."

Trey and Gideon exited the elevator on the third floor and made their way down the hallway toward the VCU office. Gideon's headache had now matured as Trey droned on about how much of a dick Nelson Diaz had been, how much of a MILF Mona was, that Diaz was definitely hiding something, and how they needed to go back to his office and press him some more. This was followed by further clarification on Mona's potential as it directly related to the prudish style of dress she had displayed in the office.

Gideon stopped just outside the VCU doorway and placed his index finger perpendicular to his mouth as he turned toward Trey.

"Trey . . . shhhh!"

Gideon pushed open the door and walked straight over to his desk, sinking heavily into the chair. As he rubbed his eyes, he saw both Eddie and Powell at their desks, both on the phone. Powell's conversation appeared to be a bit more animated, and he surmised that Ryden must have been on the other end of the line. As Powell slammed down the receiver, Gideon thought better of it but couldn't help himself.

"What's wrong, Powell?"

"Do you know what that skinny little fucker just said?" Powell snapped.

"What skinny little fucker would that be, Joe?" Gideon knew he had stoked a fire now and wished he had been a bit more rhetorical.

"We went and interviewed that McNamara prick at the news station, and the whole way there, he's giving me shit because I asked him to stop so I could get something to eat. When we're done, we get all the way back over here, and we get a call from one of the employees over there saying that there's a cameraman working there with a bunch of domestic violence arrests, or some shit like that. Jason said he'd go back over there and run it down, and since we were already back at the office, I was gonna stay here and write up what we already had."

Still rubbing his head, Gideon fought the urge and lost. "Okay, so what's the problem?"

"That little fuck just called and said he was driving by McDonald's, and saw that there were fifty-nine-cent cheeseburgers on Wednesday, and wanted to know if I wanted him to stock up for me!"

Trey cackled, and Gideon moved his hand over his mouth to cover the smile.

Powell looked around the room at both of them. "Ya know what? You two can kiss my ass, too!"

Trey looked over at Gideon. "*Well* . . . it would take both of us, ya know."

Powell jumped up from his desk as Trey turned, flung open the door, and bounded down the hallway laughing, with Joe quickly behind him. Gideon propped his feet up on the desk, still smiling, and listened as the hurried footsteps gave way to a couple of raucous thuds near the elevator—then silence.

Guess he didn't make it, Gideon thought.

Eddie dropped the receiver down onto his phone and leaned back clasping his hands behind his head.

"Well, Gideon, you're not gonna like this."

"What now?"

"I just got off the phone with the lab. Lindsay Diaz's car is a complete dead end, no pun intended. They couldn't find anything to indicate that there had been any kind of struggle there. No blood, no tissue, no hairs. Absolutely nothing."

"Okay, so what about the area where we found the body?"

"The FDLE boys found a small strip of leather under where her body was lying. That's why we didn't catch it initially. Looks like maybe a piece of a strap or something with what looks like a little bit of blood on it. They didn't do a presumptive test on it because there's not a whole lot of it, and if they do that in the field, it'll ruin the sample for a DNA test later. So I told them to hold off and just do the DNA comparison when they get back to the lab. I'm willing to bet it's her blood, but I told them to save part of the sample in case we get lucky and it's the bad guy's."

"Well, it's a start," Gideon said. "Eddie, if we haven't already, check with ViCAP and see if there's anything there that resembles what we've got. This can't be the first rodeo for this guy."

The ViCAP, or Violent Criminal Apprehension Program computer database was the FBI's preeminent nationwide clearinghouse for keeping track of known and unknown violent offenders and the mayhem that they exerted on society. In 1985, it had been constructed to track and associate information on violent crimes throughout the country including murder, kidnapping, sexual assault, and missing persons' cases where foul play had been suspected. ViCAP had gained its reputation as indispensible in tracking and comparing the signatures of serial killers around the country. Before ViCAP, a serial killer had but to change location in order to stay ahead of the law and keep his method secret. It was pure luck if different agencies from different parts of the country were ever made privy to similarities in their cases. Gideon was sure that the system would kick back something that might help point them in a direction—any direction.

"Oh yeah," Eddie said, "almost forgot. The lab guys and I went over to the morgue, and they actually pulled a partial print from the girl's throat, some iodine fuming thingie. It was pretty cool to tell you the truth."

"Is it usable?" Gideon asked.

"Probably not. They're gonna take it back to the analysts in fingerprint analysis and see if it's good enough quality for an AFIS comparison, but they said not to get your hopes up. On a happier note, if we catch this guy, the prints probably good enough for a direct comparison, though."

"Great, Eddie. So all we have to do is *catch* the guy first. Great, I feel so much better now, 'cause a couple of minutes ago it just seemed so hopeless and all."

"I do what I can, bubba," Eddie lilted, "I do what I can."

Gideon glanced at his watch and saw that it was getting late. He stood up, grabbed his keys, and walked toward the door.

"Hey, Eddie, when Trey and Powell are done beating the shit out of each other, tell the loser to go down to the records section and start checking through our old case files for something similar. Maybe even some missing persons' stuff that we haven't ever figured out."

"What do you want me to do with the winner?" Eddie said, grinning.

"Send him home. To the victor go the spoils, right?"

Gideon opened the door to the apartment and walked into the kitchen and tossed the keys on the counter. It was six o'clock, and he still had about three hours before he was supposed to be at the library to meet with Stephanie. He pulled down a glass from the cabinet and popped the cork on a 2006 Louis Jadot Pinot Noir that had been sitting on the counter. He'd always been more of a beer drinker, but Liz had turned him onto it, and although he never admitted it to her, he really kind of liked the stuff. The French did know their grapes after all.

Gideon plopped down on the couch taking a sip from the glass and staring out over the balcony at the city below. He looked over to his right and saw the picture of him and Elizabeth at Trey's Fourth of July party and quickly flipped it over.

She's working late, he thought. *How long would it take to eat a meal? She doesn't have an hour to nosh with the guy she used to love? Who am I kidding. She'd schedule a lobotomy to keep from being in the same room as me.*

Gideon placed the glass down on the floor and leaned back into the couch, closing his eyes. *Maybe a quick nap will get rid of this headache*, he thought. His eyes closed, and momentarily, the anguish of another day swept away behind him.

19

Park Avenue grew dim as day turned to night, and a light but steady rain began to empty over Tallahassee. Street lamps flickered on as shadows cast an eerie pall over the square downtown. For some reason, the rain always made it easier, he thought as he stood in the shadows near the park bench watching her through the window. In this kind of weather, people tended to stay inside, and for those who did venture out, they were more inclined to get quickly to their destinations and not pay him too much attention. Motionless, he let the rain wash down over him as he cinched his coat tighter against him. His hand stroked over the length of the cold steel blade in his pocket, and he closed his eyes for a moment, visualizing her beneath him as Ms. Finch had once been ill-fated enough to suffer.

She has no idea what she is to be a part of, the voice echoed.

"Of course she doesn't, you twit," Mathias whispered. In the years since the voice had made itself known, Mathias had grown more confident in his skills and his task, and less pliable to the will of the voice.

Do it. Do it now!

"Relax, old friend," Mathias whispered, "there is always time to watch."

She sat huddled over her desk, focused on the papers before her, a single banker's lamp casting a small halo around the small office. Twirling her dark hair around her finger, she stopped, momentarily, and looked up and removed her reading glasses and gazed out the window.

She sees you!

From inside the dimly lit room, the square outside was dark, and shapes blended seamlessly into shadows. She caught herself thinking of him and how talking to him today had actually been a pleasant surprise. She stood and walked across the room, retrieving a heavy leather book from the shelf. The thought was, however, fleeting, and she placed the book onto the desk and returned to her spot within the halo.

The voice, of course, had been wrong. She hadn't seen him. In the dark, through the rain, he would be nothing more than an apparition—a fog on the window, a bad dream to be dismissed as quickly as a waking moment.

He moved swiftly into the red brick alleyway, quietly making his way to the side door. There was no light in the alley, making it dark as pitch. He fumbled for the doorknob, finding the slip of paper he'd placed in the lock earlier in the day. He pulled on the knob, and the heavy steel door gave way as he grabbed the piece of paper and slipped inside. Eerie quiet echoed throughout the rooms as he made his way past the shelves and empty rooms and down the hallway toward the light at the other end. He stood, for a moment, in the darkened doorway of the office watching her as the light radiated low around her. Water slowly trickled off of his coat, pooling on the floor around him.

She knows not . . .

It may have been the pitter-patter sound of the water running onto the floor that caused her to look up quickly, albeit not quickly enough. His hand in his pocket grasping the steel, he closed her in seconds and snatched her up by the throat, raising her off her feet against the very window he'd spied her through, her glasses tumbling to the floor. Her legs flailed as she tried failingly to scream and as his long fingers closed tighter around her neck. She took one short gasp, and her eyes widened in horror as she saw the flash of metal, looking down at him as he plunged the blade deep into her gut and slowly, deliberately, sliced sideways in both directions. He locked his gaze to hers as the halo began to fade around her, a small trickle of blood forming at the corner of her mouth. Silently, he smiled up at her as a warmth washed over him, and he watched the life drain from her still open eyes. In another moment she was still.

The crash below startled Gideon awake, and he instinctively reached for his gun which he suddenly realized was on the counter across the room. Still half asleep, he sat up rubbing his eyes and looked down to see the wine glass lying on its side, the crimson red pool on the carpet beside it. He stared at it for a moment as an ominous feeling overcame him, and he felt a chill run down his back as he flashed back to Lindsay Diaz lying beneath the white linen sheet.

Quickly snapping back to semiconsciousness, he thought, *Damn, why couldn't she like white wine. That's gonna be a bitch to get out.*

Still dazed and unsure of what the noise had been, he stood up and crossed over the room, opening the sliding glass door and stepping out onto the balcony. He looked down on to the street below and saw the two cars mangled haplessly together. The crash had pushed both over and onto the sidewalk. Two people were staggering around the wreckage and periodically calling each other asshole. Gideon looked up when he heard the sirens and saw the red and blue lights clamoring up Pensacola Street and closing in on them. The rain had slowed to a drizzle, but people in this town were some of the worst bad weather drivers in the country. Florida rain, in any amount, apparently had the uncanny ability to cause complete and utter brain-lock when operating a motor vehicle. He had always thought it as a strange malady, but something that you just kind of got used to—like herpes.

He glanced down at his watch: 9:30.

"Shit . . . shit . . . shit!" he screamed, looking down to see the confused looks on the faces below.

"What?" Gideon yelled down at them. "That was just a really nice car, that's all!"

He stepped back inside, grabbed his gun off the counter, and quickly scrambled his way down to the parking garage. Out on the street, the accident had blocked his path on the one-way street, and he cut the corner going the wrong way over to Adams Street and swung around onto Monroe as he turned at Park Avenue and parked in front of the federal courthouse again. As he got out of the car, he glanced over across the street to Elizabeth's window. There were no lights on, and her black Camry was nowhere to be seen.

So much for working late, he thought.

He made his way down the sidewalk, running through a thousand possible excuses that Stephanie might actually buy for being a half hour late. Gideon realized that this was a professional call, but this was the same woman who had slipped an ancient sex manual into his bag and asked him to come see her after closing. Being an educated guy, he assumed that the probabilities were high for an extra-curricular nightcap. As he walked up the front steps of the library, he peered through the window but saw nothing in the darkness. He made his way around to the side door as she had instructed and rang the buzzer. After several minutes, ringing gave way to knocking and finally yelling her name—still no answer. He reached into his pocket for the phone and the slip of paper she had given him, punching in her phone number. As he stood in the shadows listening to the phone ring, that ominous feeling washed over him again as he caught the haunting opening riff of Marilyn Manson's cover of "Sweet Dreams" bellowing from a small dark sedan approaching from down the street toward Liz's office. It traveled slowly toward him, and he thought that he might have recognized it if he was just a little closer. With the phone still ringing in his hand, he walked out onto the sidewalk and into the light in the direction of the car. Suddenly the car stopped, and the song's melody grew eerily louder as Gideon strained to see who might be inside. As the song faded, the car slowly turned left away from him and disappeared down South Adams Street.

Gideon thought briefly about chasing after, but thought that he'd had just about enough creepy shit for one evening. After no answer at Stephanie's house, he snapped the phone shut and made his way back to the car. As he headed back to the apartment, he turned down Adams but caught no sight of the dark sedan. He wasn't sure why it mattered. It was probably nothing anyway, and after all, he couldn't even tell what kind of car it was in the first place. The song reverberated in his head, though, and he couldn't shake the uneasy feeling it gave him. This had undoubtedly been a fairly creepy week anyway. Maybe it was just Liz leaving her office, and he had simply missed her as he passed by. That would explain why she drove away when he stepped out into the light, he thought. He flipped open the phone and brought her number up on speed dial. After another moment, he thought better of it and flipped the phone shut without dialing as he eased back home.

Back at the apartment, he kicked off his shoes and tossed the gun and keys on the counter. He walked around and picked up the wine glass and saw the stain was now good and set in the carpet. It had darkened some and looked more like blood than it had before. Gideon placed the glass on the counter and grabbed the bottle, collapsing down on the couch. He took a long swig and leaned back, closing his eyes, the headache still with him.

I really gotta think about trying yoga or something, he thought.

At 2:30, the phone rang again. The empty wine bottle rolled off onto the floor as Gideon reached on top of the couch, flipping it open.

"Kane . . ."

"Gideon, we got another one . . . and this one's bad."

"Geez, Trey . . . bad? What would call the last one?"

"Just get down here, Gideon. This is one you're gonna want to be at personally. We're at McCarthy Park, outside Liz's office."

"Elizabeth!" Gideon yelled. "Is she . . . ?"

"Just get down here, buddy. We'll talk about it when you get here."

"Trey! Is she . . . ?" The phone went dead.

Gideon brought Elizabeth up on speed dial and pressed the button. After several rings, the call went to her voicemail. He didn't leave a message because he knew she never checked it anyway. He tried it again—same thing. He grabbed his gun, slipped on his shoes, and clambered out the door.

20

Gideon raced the Impala through the winding passageways of the garage. As he neared the entrance, he hoped that the accident scene had been cleared because he wasn't stopping, and he figured that he was gonna need the extra space to make the turn. As he burst almost airborne from the garage and out onto Bronough Street and back around the corner to the left, he was amazed—as the smoke from the tires cleared—that there had been no traffic at all. He blew the light at College Avenue and came screeching around the corner to East Park. Trey was standing near the bench outside Elizabeth's office, and he saw the emergency lights bouncing off of the familiar white linen sheet draped over it as he came running over. Gideon quickly grabbed the edge of the sheet where he saw the hair tumbling out from underneath—and suddenly felt himself unable to move. After a moment, he looked over at Trey, and then back down. He took a deep breath and slowly drew back the sheet, revealing her face. Gideon felt *that* chill as he shuddered falling to his knees, the image of the dark sedan flashing before him.

Trey moved over to him quickly. "Gideon . . . you okay?" he asked. "You know her or something?"

Gideon sank from his knees, sitting down on the ground, arms around his knees as he stared up at the sheet.

"Her name is Stephanie . . . She worked in the library over there," he muttered, crestfallen. "I was supposed to meet her over there at about nine last night, but I was late . . . and she never showed.

"Meet her? What for?"

Gideon took another deep breath. "Lillian clued me in a book that might be related to the Diaz murder . . . a very *old* book. Stephanie was gonna sneak me in after they closed and let me get a peek at their records . . . to see who's checked it out before."

"So let me get this straight," Trey snapped, pointing toward the sheet. "This girl . . . this *dead* girl *right here,* was gonna help you break into the library and steal private records. Then she stands you up, and five hours later, we find her dead on a park bench across the street, split open like a . . . a . . . turducken!"

"Turducken?" Gideon echoed.

"Yeah, turducken . . . You know, they cut open a turkey and then a duck and a chicken. Then they put the duck inside the turkey, and the chicken inside the duck, then they wrap the whole thing up and cook it."

Gideon sat staring at him silently with a quizzical look.

Trey paused for a moment. "It's actually quite tasty, ya know, even though it doesn't sound like it."

Gideon closed his eyes as his head dropped down to his knees. After a moment, he popped his head up, confused.

"Wait a minute . . . whaddya mean cut open?"

"Dude, she was split from hip to hip. Some kind of short blade, I think. There's not a lot of tearing either, so whatever it was, it was pretty damn sharp. A razor maybe."

"Show me," Gideon said, rising quickly up.

Trey moved over and pulled back the sheet even further. Her dark suit helped to absorb and hide most of the blood, but the wound was unmistakable against the white shirt. The body was becoming distended, forcing slightly the insides out through the hole, making an examination of the wound edges difficult, and the rain had distorted the fabric against her skin. Trey had been right, though. The edges of the shirt where the weapon had cut through were smooth, very smooth, except for the extreme left edge.

"Here," Gideon said, pointing to it. "See where this is pushed in and torn? He stuck her first, *and then* sliced over. This isn't a slash." He turned back to Trey. "How many straight razors have you seen that had a sharpened tip?"

Trey processed the thought, arching his eyebrows. "Well . . . there *is* that . . . " After a moment, he continued, "How 'bout a scalpel?"

Gideon nodded affirmatively. "Anyone checked the eyes yet?"

"Nope. Her hair's matted all over her face . . . almost like he pulled it down to cover it up."

Gideon grabbed the pen from Trey's hand and moved toward the other end of the bench. Leaning over her, he began clearing the wet hair from her eyes. In a moment, his answer was clear.

"Gone," he said.

"Gone?" Trey echoed.

"Gone. There's some bruising around her throat, too. Make sure the lab gets a look at that. Eddie said they were able to lift a partial print off of Lindsay. Maybe we'll get lucky here, too."

Trey leaned over to look at her throat and glanced up at her face, noticing what looked like a cut above her eye partially protruding from under the remaining matted hair.

"I thought you said this guy was clean when he removed the eyes, Gideon? Looks like there's some peripheral damage here."

Gideon leaned back down and, using the pen, nudged the remaining hair away from her forehead as recognizable symbols began to emerge.

"He carved a message into her forehead!" Trey said abruptly. "This guy's a fuckin' gem, I tell you. You suppose maybe it's his name and address?"

Trey grabbed another pen from his pocket and began writing down the letters as he spoke them aloud, "A – E – G – R – I . . . S – O – M – N – I – A."

Trey looked down at his pad, trying poorly to make sense of it. "What the hell does this mean? It looks like the leftover board from Wheel of Fortune."

Gideon looked down at the pad, and the chill overtook him again as recognition set in. "It's Latin," he said.

"When did you learn to speak Latin?"

"I did go to college, ya know," Gideon said. "And Liz, being a lawyer and all, it was always kind of . . . *around*, so I sorta just picked up bits and pieces here and there. Besides, you don't really *speak* Latin. It sounds too screwy. It's actually more suited to a *read-only* kind of thing."

"Okay, Pluto . . . so what does it say?"

"You mean Plato, right?" Gideon responded.

"Whatever!" Trey barked. "What does it say?"

Gideon stood silent for a moment, staring from the pad then back over to her face, wishing suddenly that he hadn't been able to read the message.

"Gideon!" Trey pleaded. "What?"

Gideon slowly spoke, "A sick man's dream . . . It says *a sick man's dream.*"

"Yeah, no shit! He didn't have to carve it into her fucking forehead for me to pull that shit outta there!"

Gideon turned, handing the pen back to Trey who grabbed it before realizing, and dropped it again almost as quickly.

"Trey, let's get her outta the rain already, okay? She doesn't deserve any more of this. And let's wake up the head library guy and see if we've got a secondary crime scene. Put some marked units over there until he gets here to open it up."

"Taken care of, Gideon."

Gideon inched closer, pulled the sheet back up over her, and began walking back to the car. He stopped briefly, looking up at Elizabeth's window, smiling and feeling a little glad that she'd lied about working late—else it'd be her on that bench. The image of the dark sedan flashed again in his mind, and he wondered if that had been the killer, or if he had been that close and missed him, or if Stephanie had been lying on the bench when he got back in his car only thirty feet away. *What if he hadn't been late?* he thought. Would she still be alive? And why *her* in the first place? Did it have something to do with their meeting, something about that damn book? In any event, he knew that things were going to be bad in the morning, and the press was going to have a field day with this one. Two mutilated women in a week was not going to play well on the news, and when your boss is an elected official, that meant pressure. Gideon knew that a trip to the fourth floor was inevitable now.

I hope they got a lot *of that green carpet up there*, he thought.

21

Knowing sleep was not in his near future, Gideon drove back over to the VCU office while Trey made arrangements for getting into the library. As he opened the office door, he saw Powell hunched over, asleep on his desk, and Gideon did his best not to wake him. He sat down quietly and powered up the computer as he sat staring out the window, Powell snoring across the way like a white noise machine. A picture of Elizabeth mocked him from the corner of his desk, and he flipped it down on its face. It wasn't the first time he'd turned it over, and it probably wouldn't be the last. All at once, he felt wholly pathetic.

The hourglass stopped spinning as the computer came to life, and he spent some time googling "zeis." After playing around with a few different spelling variations, he clicked on a *Wikipedia* article about Carl Zeiss, a nineteenth century German optician. As he half-heartedly continued, not expecting to find much, he discovered that Zeiss's legacy had lived on through Carl Zeiss Incorporated, a German company that produced high quality optics, including camera lenses, binoculars, and rifle scopes.

"Holy shit! They're binoculars!" Gideon screamed, as a muffled grunt and a heavy thud traveled across the room. Gideon looked over at him as Powell pulled himself up off the floor and righted his chair.

"What the fuck are you trying to do, kill me?" Joe said.

"The two circles on her back . . . the strip of leather at the scene," Gideon belted, "don't you get it Joe? They're binoculars!"

"And? That tells us what? That she had binoculars when she died? Holy Christ, Gideon, you've done it! You've cracked the fuckin case! I'll call Priceline, and we can get a couple o' tickets to Germany so we can go arrest this Zeiss motherfucker and we can all go home!"

Gideon paused for a moment, not sure if he was supposed to be pissed or if Powell was right.

Powell continued, "Now, just do me one more favor since you're gettin' so excited about shit, Sherlock. Who killed Kennedy? I'm just askin' 'cause you're on a roll and everything. Oh, and while we're at it, who was the fuckin' genius that decided that bringing *Knight Rider* back to television without David Hasselhoff was a good idea . . . 'cause I tell you, that's the asshole I wanna put in fuckin' jail!"

Again, Gideon paused, this time it was actually because, he, too, had always wondered how you could do *Knight Rider* without the Hoffmeister.

"You haven't eaten, have you?" Gideon said. "What are you still doing here anyway, Joe?"

"I tripped at the elevator on that damn green carpet out there, and Trey got a lucky punch in."

"Ohh . . . so you're the one who lost."

"I didn't lose, I tripped! Anyway, I've spent the last few hours going over cold cases and some old shit that's been inactive for years."

"And . . . ?" Gideon reciprocated.

"Well, actually, there's been quite a few missing persons cases that we haven't ever closed. More than I would expect for this town. Never mind me, what are you doing here?"

"We just caught another one, Joe," said Gideon.

"Another one? Where . . . who?"

"McCarthy Park. She worked at the library. She was supposed to get up with me tonight and give me some records that might have helped, but I was late. Then Trey called and said they found her across the street in the park."

"You knew her?"

"I didn't *know* her, but I'd met her a few times."

Powell stared at him, arching his right eyebrow as if waiting for a further clarification.

"That's all!" Gideon snapped.

Powell's eyebrow dropped. "Whatever . . ."

Gideon continued, "Same MO as the Diaz girl. Except this one had her gut slit open."

"Really?" Powell said rhetorically. "Nothin' like up close and personal for upping the scare factor."

"Whaddya mean?"

"Well, I read some of your case notes on the Diaz kid, and I agree that this ain't his first one . . . just the first one we know about. This one have any symbols?"

"Yeah," Gideon said, "she had 'sick man's dream' on her forehead."

"What the hell is that supposed to mean?"

"I dunno," Gideon said plaintively, "but you gotta admit, it fits."

"Okay, so he sticks around the dead body long enough to take the eyes, carve a message, and open up her gut. But on the first one, he took the time to knock her out first, sew the mouth shut, not to mention moving the body to a secondary scene. A *remote* secondary scene."

"Okay, so where are you going with this?" Gideon asked.

"Well, you've got to admit that McCarthy Park is not the least bit remote, and the mouth wasn't stitched up or anything, right?"

"Right."

"So he goes through all of that, twice, mind you, *forgets* to close the mouth, *and* only moves her across the street? Powell began shaking his head. "Dude . . . he wasn't done. He was interrupted."

"Interrupted?"

"Yeah, I'm assuming that the park was only a secondary dump scene."

"Probably didn't look like enough blood there for it to have been the initial."

"And," Powell added, "you don't split somebody in two like that without them making some noise . . . noise which would have been very noticeable in a downtown park with busy roads on all four sides. Somebody cut him off Gideon. He wasn't finished."

"Me," Gideon whispered.

"You?"

"I was supposed to meet her down at the library at nine, but I didn't get there until nine thirty. She told me to go to the side door, but she never showed."

"So then what'd you do?"

"I started walking back to my car, but I noticed this other car on the way . . . gave me a creepy kinda vibe."

"Where was the car?"

"Actually, it was coming from right around where the body was found," Gideon said. "And it stopped when I came from around the building. When I started walking toward it, it just disappeared down Adams Street. Couldn't tell you anything about it, other than I remember thinking it was Liz's car at first. But she wouldn't have gone that way to go home, not to mention that I like to think she would have stopped and said something."

Gideon sat up and leaned forward, in thought, for a moment and turned back to Powell.

"Anyway, what were you saying about the old case files?"

Powell turned the chair and sat down, grabbing a few files from the stack on his desk and rolled over closer to Gideon.

"Listen, Sarge, you know how ninety-nine percent of these runaways and missing persons are usually just some kid who needs a break from their parents or some manic-depressive who just needs to get away for a few hours, right?"

"Yeah, so?"

"Well, we usually solve those within a week, or thereabouts, so they're filed as closed and solved. Only problem is that over the past ten years or so, we've had about four of these a year that are still open. We haven't found them yet . . . no trace, and they're all legitimate skips too. There's no reason any of them should have gone missing in the first place. Even weirder part is, they all happened about the same time of the month . . . roughly the first ten days, give or take a day."

"Okay," Gideon said, "so what does that have to do with this?"

"Well, maybe nothing at all, but one of those cases, the first one in fact, was a woman named Abigail Arbin."

"Who the hell is Abigail Arbin?"

"I had a problem, at first, putting it all together because she was *actually found* down in Wakulla back in 1983 . . . three weeks after she went missing, but they still had the case open."

Gideon leaned back in his chair, not following. "Okay, Joe," he asked, "I'm still not seeing the connection here."

Powell continued, "There was a pretty good car accident back in '83 between this lady and a logging truck. Long story short, the car goes off a bridge into the Wakulla river . . . only there's nobody in the car when they pull it out."

"So she got thrown out, and the current washed her away," Gideon posed.

"Well, that would make sense except for one teensy little problem."

"How teensy?" asked Gideon.

"She washed up near a canoe rental place in Wakulla three weeks later . . . without her eyes."

"Yeah . . . I could see how that might be a problem. Maybe the fish got to 'em."

"Nope, not the fish. Fish would've eaten away the soft tissue around the eyelids to get to them. Other than the eyes . . . and, of course, a broken neck . . . she was pristine for someone who'd spent three weeks in the river."

"So . . . what," Gideon offered, "she washes on shore for a while, and then the tide comes up and pulls her back in. A floater from twenty-five years ago does not make a serial killer, Joe."

"Still doesn't explain the eyes," Powell said, leaning in. "Someone pulled her out, took her eyes, and kept her dry for a while before they put her back in, Gideon. That's my point. She *hadn't* been in the water for three weeks!"

Well . . . there was that, Gideon thought.

He stood as the phone in his pocket began to buzz, and he pulled it out to see Trey's number flashing again.

"All right, Joe, ya sold me. Find out everything that we don't already know about this lady, and get the records from the highway patrol about the accident and whoever worked the crash from our agency . . . maybe they can shed some light on this."

Gideon flicked the phone open. "Whatcha got for me, Trey?"

"The library guy is here with the keys, but I wanted to wait till you got back before we go in."

"I'll be there in a few," Gideon said. "Me and Powell are wrapping up some interesting cold case stuff."

"Powell?" Trey said. "He tell you that he lost?"

"Actually, he said he tripped."

"Shit! I clotheslined his ass when he came around the corner to the elevator. That boy is way too big to fight fair, Gideon."

Gideon smiled and flipped the phone shut looking over at Powell, saying nothing.

"I tripped!" Powell iterated. "That's my story, and I'm stickin' to it."

Gideon snickered as he grabbed his keys and made his way out the door and down the hallway. As he neared the corner by the elevator, he stopped, crouched low, and peeked around the corner before making the turn.

"You asshole!" boomed from behind as he looked back to see Powell standing in the doorway shaking his head. Gideon laughed as he pushed the button to call the elevator and stepped inside. The phone buzzed again, and he answered.

"Kane."

"Hey, Gideon, it's Laura."

"Hi, Doc. Lemme guess . . ."

"Eight thirty good for you?" she said, mocking him.

"Wouldn't have it any other way, Doc," he replied, snapping the phone shut.

Gideon stood silent for a moment staring at the stainless steel doors: *Always so fucking early . . .*

22

Gideon hopped into the car and made his way down a mostly desolate Pensacola Street and headed back toward downtown. As he passed by Doak Campbell Stadium, he spied two blithe coeds dancing around the statue of Bobby Bowden, hanging from his outstretched pointing hand and snapping pictures of each other, giving him kisses on the cheek with a dime-store disposable camera. For the first time in a very long time, it occurred to him that not everyone in this city was privy to its underbelly, and that for the most part, despite the unrelenting misery that a small few conveyed upon the many, life went on, and people moved forward. The fish wrap's daily headlines were, more often than not, filled with car crashes and bank robberies, meaningless shootings, and unprovoked beatings of the homeless by well-to-do kids who were simply too bored and no longer content with the on-demand violence provided by their Xbox. It occurred to him that despite two incredibly violent murders within the last few days, here were two young women who would not be deprived of some harmless late-night college revelry. The average people of this city, like every other, read these headlines with the requisite sympathy for those affected, but with their own busy lives and personal agendas, sympathy quickly gave way to apathy and ambivalence.

The fact of the matter was that while most people wanted to know the gory details, they *wanted* to forget them as soon afterward as possible. The "not-me-not-here" mentality was a necessary defense mechanism that allowed them to contend with the presence of pure evil in their perfect little worlds. Gideon and the rest of the VCU, unfortunately, did not have that luxury. For them, sympathy would inevitably morph into an empathy which could only come from injecting oneself into the darkest parts of that very evil you relentlessly begged your God to forget. All the while, your own hectic lives and dismissive ex-spouses sat perpetually on hold, only helping to carve a path to the inescapable and utter collapse into a bottle and the compulsory bouts of depression which always seemed to accompany it when you needed it the least.

As he pulled up to the library, Gideon theorized that while his particular pathway was being painstakingly whittled away for him by the likes of Lindsay Diaz, Stephanie, and Elizabeth, he still had a little borrowed time before the prostration became irreversible, and finding this crazy motherfucker would most certainly help.

He parked in the street in front of the main entrance and spied Trey standing just inside the portico talking to a smallish bespectacled man wearing baggy blue jeans that were creased down the front of each leg, a pair of yellow New Balance running shoes that were obviously well past their thirty-thousand-mile warranty, and a long-sleeved gray T-shirt emblazoned with Tulane Law running down the length of each sleeve. Gideon thought this guy definitely looked a bit more bookish than Stephanie could have ever hoped to be as he nervously fumbled with an enormous ring of keys, dropping it twice. While it was unmistakably hot outside, it was obvious that Trey had conveyed the urgency of the situation to the man as the heavy beads of sweat began to burst forth from the top of his balding head, only to slide down and disappear again beneath the poorest excuse for a reddish comb-over that Gideon could recall. As he got closer, Gideon noticed that Trey was becoming visibly more agitated with the gentleman, which in turn seemed to make the man noticeably more nervous.

"Gentlemen," Gideon piped up.

"Gideon," Trey said anxiously, his eyebrows arched in perceived disbelief, "this is Mr. Stiles, the head librarian."

"Herman Stiles," he said, extending his right hand toward Gideon and dropping the keys for a third time. "Sorry about that," he muttered, bending down to retrieve the key ring. "Actually, my official title is chief archivist."

Trey spun around, throwing his hands in the air, both slapping down heavily atop his head.

"I'm sorrrry," Trey droned mockingly, looking over at Gideon. "Herman is the chief archivist, my bad. Anyway, the keymaster here has been trying to figure out exactly which of these fifty thousand keys actually gets us in the front door for the last twenty minutes! Does that about sum it up . . . Chief?"

"I apologize, again, profusely gentlemen," Stiles said sheepishly. "It's just that the police make me nervous, and you guys . . . well, you are rather large and imposing and, uhh . . . here, I think it's this one." Shaking, he extended the key toward Trey as it suddenly slipped from his grasp and clanged against the ground in an indescribable pile.

Trey went limp, eyes closed, his chin dropped sharply against his chest. Gideon laughed quietly and put his arm around Trey, guiding him away from Stiles for a moment.

"Honestly, Gideon, how many fucking doors could there be in there! It's not the Smithsonian for Christ's sake . . . who needs that many damn keys anyway?"

"I know. There there," Gideon said, placating him as sarcastically as he knew how.

"I mean . . . I just wanna twist his goddamn head off, ya know?" Trey whispered, sounding almost despondent. "Twenty bucks says he still lives with his mother, and there's plastic on all the furniture!"

"Give him a minute there, tiger," Gideon said smirking. "Maybe he can figure it out without you towering all over him . . . you large and *imposing* beast you."

"Very funny."

"Listen," Gideon continued, "Jernigan called and set the autopsy for later this morning. Don't suppose I could talk you into going in my place, could I?"

"Nahh, those things are always so damn early in the morning, ya know?"

"Really? I never noticed over the smell."

"Besides, I've got the shooting review board this morning at eight-thirty for those SWAT guys. Hey, ya think it would be too crass if I picked up a latte and brought it with me to that?"

"Huh?"

"You know," Trey said rolling his eyes, "a latte . . . coffee shop . . . disgruntled drive-through patrons with automatic weapons and body armor . . . get it?"

Gideon finally caught on and began to laugh as the muted impish voice beckoned to them from behind.

"Here it is!" Stiles shrieked, giggling as he slid the key effortlessly into the lock, opened the door, and quickly shuffled inside, motioning them to follow. As they stepped inside, Stiles flicked the switch, and the fluorescents began to buzz and pop to life.

"Where's the office?" Trey asked sharply.

"Back behind the front reception desk and to the right," Stiles said as he began to amble in that direction.

"Stop," Gideon ordered, "you stay here until we've had a chance to clear the rest of the building. Wouldn't want you disturbing anything that I might need in court a year from now."

Stiles stopped rigidly in his tracks. "Okay, guys . . . but if the office is still locked, I'll have the keys right here if you need them."

Trey stopped, looked over at Gideon, bit his lip, and then reconsidered. "Herman . . . why don't you get a head start on that very thing right now, okay? Just in case."

"Check!" Stiles shouted as he pitched a half-hearted salute their way.

"Dude," Trey whispered to Gideon, "I'm telling you . . . plastic on the furniture, man . . . I'm never wrong about these sorts of things."

They made their way back behind the desk and turned right down the short, still darkened, hallway until they came to the exit door out into the east alley. Trey knelt down and spread the beam from his flashlight low across the floor as the watery footprints glistened against the tile, tiny dark specks dotted the dry areas between them.

"Could be blood," Trey whispered.

"Why are you whispering?"

"Because he could still be in there."

"We just turned on all the lights, and there's been, like a thousand cop cars outside for hours. I don't think we're gonna sneak up on him!"

"Well, there's that I suppose."

They carefully moved against the right edge of the hallway, avoiding disturbing any of the footprints, and approached the office door which was already ajar, a dim light showing upward through the crack from somewhere near the floor. Gideon drew his Glock pistol and, hugging the wall, eased the door open further, scanning the corners of the room before stepping inside and moving to the right side of the doorway. Trey followed immediately, sliding left to cover the other half of the room, and flipped on the overhead light switch. As he moved slowly behind the desk, he saw the banker's lamp lying on the floor beneath the window, a dark pool of liquid lay beneath. It struck him as if someone had poured a couple quarts of motor oil in a pool below.

Gideon looked up to the window and saw the small bloody handprints smeared across its face, starting up high before sliding down toward the bottom of the sill. As he shuffled around to the opposite side of the desk and noticed the antique Seth Thomas mantel clock lying on the floor, its crystal and bezel cracked, the hands read 9:01.

"Fuck me!" Gideon screamed, collapsing back into the chair behind him.

"What?"

"I was supposed to be here at nine. The clock stopped a minute after that . . . if I wasn't late . . ."

"You can't do that, Gideon. You didn't create this . . . *he* did!"

Gideon rubbed his eyes and stared back up at the handprints on the window, images of Stephanie's last moments flashing before him.

"I know, man," Gideon uttered, "it's just that all this pain is getting kind of old."

Gideon stood, still staring at the window.

"So how'd the prints get all the way up there?" he said. "She wasn't an inch over five three."

"He picked her up?"

"Up there? If he held her up there, he's a big man. Even a hundred and twenty pounds is a bitch to keep up that high when it's kicking and screaming . . . especially with one hand."

"How'd you know it was one hand?"

"All that blood on the floor right underneath . . . that's where he gutted her. Had to have a hand free to do that, right? Held her there and watched her too . . . watched her while she bled out."

"And we know this because . . . ?"

"Those specks in the hallway . . . you're telling me he slices her open, and there's no more blood in the hallway than that?"

"How long you think it would it have taken her to bleed out like that?" Trey queried.

"Longer than you or I could have held her there . . . or both of us together for that matter. Who the fuck *is* this guy?"

Gideon began to walk back toward the door when he spotted a glint from something lying on the back edge of the desk.

"What is that?" he asked.

Trey inched over, grabbed a glove from his pocket, and used it to pick up the object.

"Looks like a button . . . heavy though."

"Why's all the stuff on the desk lying on the floor, but there's no blood?" Gideon asked.

"Yeah, that doesn't make a whole lot of sense considering all the blood is pooled under the window."

Gideon walked over and grabbed the glove from Trey, examining the button for a moment, and then looking back over the desktop.

"He dove at her . . . or jumped across, caught her by surprise."

"The button's his, then?"

"Let's check the body . . . her clothes. Make sure it's not hers. If it doesn't match, then he's made his first mistake."

Trey wrapped the button inside the glove, and the two of them moved back out into the hallway. Edging back down the hall avoiding the footprints, they made their way to the exit door. Gideon grabbed another glove from his pocket and gently turned the handle, nudging the door open slightly. Trey moved in beside him and turned his light toward the doorway as Gideon bent down closer to examine the lock.

"No pry marks . . . not a scratch," he said as he reached around to check the handle from the outside. "And the door's still locked from the inside."

"Well," Trey chimed in, "maybe he came in when the place was still open and waited until everyone left."

"Then we wouldn't have the wet footprints, though."

"So how'd he get in the door without prying it then?"

"He either rigged it somehow, or he came in the normal way and unlocked it. Either way, he had to come inside at some point while they were open, to do it."

"I'm not seeing him take the time to re-lock the door on the way out. What would be the point? You're not hiding anything in here. You've already taken the body outside to be found. He had to know we end up here at some point."

"True enough," Gideon said. "Like I said, either way he was inside the building during office hours. Let's get with Stiles and see if this place has any video and get crime scene in here, and if they don't do anything else, make sure they dust the hell out of that door and the lock. Maybe we'll get a little lucky."

"All right, where you headed to?"

"I've just got something nagging at me. Gotta check on something. Make sure everything's okay, that's all. I'll see you later today."

Gideon eased out the side door, using his elbow so as not to disturb any potential prints around the lock. This exit also facilitated his ability to avoid Stiles. He cranked up the Impala and pointed north, a short distance down Monroe Street, and took the exit to Thomasville Road. At this time of night, traffic was more or less lacking, and he was in Killearn in less than ten minutes. He turned off the headlights as he turned onto the side street lined tightly with very tiny lots on which were packed very tiny houses. As he pulled in front of the house, he saw her car in the driveway and felt relief that she'd made it home okay after all.

"Just checkin', honey," he whispered quietly to himself. He turned the headlights back on as he pulled away and headed back home for a couple of hours of shut-eye before the autopsy. The thought hit him like a brick as he pulled back out onto the main road: *There was no other car in the driveway . . . that was a good sign . . .*

23

Mathias stopped short in the driveway and pressed the button on the visor overhead, the ambient sounds of the metal door clanking to life, a welcome alternative from the incessant droning of the voice in his head.

You shouldn't have fled . . . there was time!

"No!" he snapped. "There was not."

The act was not complete! There was more work to be done!

"We have what we came for! Why must you always nag me so?"

There are rules, *dear boy . . . ways and means of doing things. The soul is an evanescent being . . . capricious and difficult to control.*

The door fully opened, Mathias eased the car gently into the garage, pressing the button a second time. Immobile, he watched as the door returned, sweeping the moonlight back outside behind him.

"We have what we need," he repeated.

She would always listen to me . . . obey as she was told before she crossed over.

It was the first time that the voice had made reference to her, and it did not sit well with him. It had finally occurred to him that he was not alone. She had been privy to his rants as well and passed the burden down upon his shoulders.

"There was no way to know that he would have been there," Mathias responded.

Then we would have taken care of him as well, boy!

"If he were to have seen us, all our work would have been for naught!"

As I said, child, then he would join the others . . . you are letting him get too close!

"How . . . how is he getting close? He knows nothing!"

Ahh . . . but he suspects. Something nags at him . . . he is unsure what it is, but it haunts him . . . pushes him further along to finding the answers he seeks . . . you should not have followed him yesterday. It is now only a matter of time before he unmasks us.

"Why do you taunt me?"

Because you insist on ignoring me, child . . . and because I can . . .

He fumbled in the dark for the handle, his hands still sticky from the evening's tasks, and stepped from the car. A thin wisp of light crept through the crack in the pantry door from the kitchen, guiding him. As he stepped into the pantry, he removed the small glass vial and the blade from the pocket of his coat, placed them on the thin wooden shelf above, and lifted open the lid of the washing machine. Turning the knob to start the cycle, he began to undress, tossing the items inside, the heat of the water igniting the sickly sweet smell of the dried blood which wafted up over him. He leaned his head over and took a deep breath of the perfume as he closed his eyes, a faint smile forming as if at peace. As the water finished rushing in and the cycle started, he closed the lid and gazed down at himself standing bare as the light reflected up at him against his pale skin, smears and specks of reddish-brown covering his wrists and hands. He reached up and took the vial from the shelf and walked through the kitchen to the door opening into the backyard. As he stepped outside, the volume of the cicadas chirping drowned out the voice as he made his way across the grass to the shed.

The door creaked as it opened, and he stepped inside and flipped the switch as the fluorescents flickered to life. Mathias walked slowly over to the workbench and gazed over the rows of jars lining the overhead shelf two-deep, each with their own all too familiar story. All had met their end at his hand. Some knew him, others did not, but all would know him in the end. This was where they all ended up. This is where the road ended: their final vision before crossing over—a dark and dank wooden storage shed with a dirt floor in a remote part of the county along the river. He turned and held the vial up to the light, squinting slightly and admiring the orbs as they insinuated a return gaze at him.

They're magnificent, aren't they?

"Truly," he replied.

We are so close now, child . . . but you must hurry, and that policeman is not far off, I believe. Only one more to go, and we will finally be ready for the rapture.

Mathias turned back, making a space on the end of the shelf for the new addition. The smile faded from his face as Murmur's words hung thickly in the air around him.

"One more," he whispered.

He pushed the switch as the light abruptly escaped, and he walked back outside, closing the door behind him. The moonlight against his skin turned the blood on his hands black, and he turned them over and over, staring and seduced by the warmth it provided him. After a moment, he walked back up into the house and prepared himself a warm tub, the water becoming opaque as he lie down in the water, the blood releasing from his skin. His eyes fell shut as he lie still, slinking down slightly, bringing his ears below the water. Perhaps this would prevent the voice from disturbing him. As the sounds of the washing machine ebbed away from downstairs—he dreamed.

24

The rain had eased slightly overnight to a persistent and annoying drizzle. The kind that sits just in-between two settings on the windshield wipers, but as Gideon pulled into the parking garage of the hospital, the skies began to empty. He shook his coat as he stepped from the car and hurried through the breezeway and into the lobby. Another amazing day to be thankful for—kicked off with the dissection of yet another lost soul. Another letdown to add to the countless ones before that he hadn't been there to protect. It didn't matter that there would have been no way to predict it, no way to head it off. That wasn't the point. Gideon, like any good homicide cop, hated to lose—even if the deck was stacked against him.

He stepped off the elevator and made his way slowly down the hallway in none too much of a hurry. He couldn't even come close to remembering how many of these he had been to. The majority of the people in the upper floors of the hospital had no idea that there was a morgue in the basement. He, unfortunately, did. It often gave him the creeps thinking of himself lying on that cold steel table when he had finally finished his own theme park ride through life—a ride that was currently at the top of the coaster and about to go over the other side to that endless drop that seems to go straight down, and you can't help wonder how it manages to stay on the tracks. Despite all the others, this would be the first in which he had actually known the person lying on the table, the first that he had interacted with and spoken to. *This was gonna suck*, he thought.

At the end of the hallway, he peeked into Jernigan's empty office, her coffee cup still steaming on the desk. He turned slightly toward the empty coat rack outside the door and peeled off the black Pronto Uomo raincoat that Elizabeth had given him last Christmas. An Uomo coat was not an item conducive to the average cop's salary, but Elizabeth had always had great taste in clothes. Before she had come along, his idea of rainwear would have been a magazine or newspaper held over his head as he sprinted for anyplace dry. She had told him once that perception was reality, and one's appearance was most definitely the perception.

He placed the coat on the hook and leaned against the wall for a moment, taking a deep breath. As he exhaled, he grabbed the handle and pushed through the door into the lab. Jernigan was standing on her step stool at the table over Stephanie's body, whispering into her microcassette recorder and delivering the pre-op notes before beginning the procedure.

"Hey, Doc," he said uneasily, "what's cookin'?"

"Steak tartare this morning, Gideon," she said wryly. "Care to help me in the kitchen?"

It hadn't ever occurred to him that Laura actually had a sense of humor, and yet for a moment, she was just as sick as he was. It was somewhat comforting.

"C'mon, Laura, you know I can't cook."

"Good thing it's tartare then, huh?" she scoffed. "Now get over here and help me. Mattie's running late, and I really could use a third hand."

She grabbed an extra face shield and gown and tossed them onto the counter beside him.

"Get those on," she said, "and do me a favor and grab the pruning shears from the bucket over there, okay?"

Gideon suddenly felt nauseous and dizzy, and he clung tightly to the counter to steady himself.

"You okay, Gideon?" she asked as she turned and stepped off the stool. "What's the matter? You're not gettin' soft on me, are you?"

"It's not that, Doc . . . I just . . . "

"You knew her ,didn't you?" she said, plopping down on the counter stool, realizing her mistake.

"Great, the one time *I* make a joke to *you*, and it blows up in my face. Don't I feel like quite the shit at the moment?"

Gideon looked up at her. "Is that a rhetorical question or what?"

The tension eased for a moment, and they both began to smile. Laura reached out and placed her hand on his trembling arm.

"Are you sure you're okay, Gideon? You don't have to stay if it's going to be too much."

"I'm fine. I just haven't had a lot of sleep lately . . . what with this case and the divorce and all."

"That's right, I almost forgot," she said. "How is Elizabeth these days?"

"I really couldn't tell you, Laura. We don't talk much anymore."

"Really, why is that?"

"Again, your guess is as good as mine."

"You know, for a detective, you don't have a whole lot of answers," she said, her smile growing.

"Listen, I appreciate the concern, but if you don't mind, can we just get through this one? I'd rather not draw it out."

"Sure, Gideon, I'm sorry . . ."

"No, really, it's okay. To be honest with you, I just haven't ever seen anyone on that slab before that I could actually remember talking to at some point in my life. It's just a little fuckin' creepy, that's all."

"Understood," she said. "Come here and take a look at this. I was going over the wound patterns before you got here, some interesting stuff actually."

Gideon grabbed a disposable mask from the counter and placed it over his face as he inched slowly closer to the exam table. The smells in this room were always bad, but he'd never needed to resort to the mask before. This time, however, was different. He just didn't want to remember Stephanie that way.

"Whatcha got?" Gideon asked, his voice muffled through the cloth.

"There's a proximal lateral puncture here on the left," she said, pointing, "or rather, *her* right side. Not too deep. I'd say about a half an inch, but enough to nick the appendix. From there, there's a ventral incision that moves medially, and continues all the way across just below the navel."

"So is it one motion, or did he stab and then slash after that?"

"Well, if you look closer here," she said, leaning down and pulling the lower flap of the abdomen outward, "you see how the skin looks to be sliced at sort of an upward angle from the fatty tissue all the way up to the epidermis?"

"Sort of, and this tells us what? Remember, Doc, I'm just a cop. You're the doctor. So far, the only word you've used that I recognize is *navel*."

Jernigan sighed and smiled as she turned toward him.

"Okay, look at it like this," she said, grabbing his wrist and pushing his shirt sleeve up, exposing his forearm. "If I slice down on your arm here, depending on the sharpness of the blade of course, it will cut through the upper layer of skin, causing tearing of the epidermal layer at the initial point of contact, however, if I continue to drag that blade across the skin without changing the depth, you won't have the same level of tearing across the length of the cut that you did at the beginning."

"Okay, I'll bite . . . why not?"

"Because our skin is pretty resilient, even elastic at younger ages. How do you think Botox works so well?"

"Okay, I get the point. So what happened here, then?"

"Well," she said, turning back toward the table, "the damage to the outer layers of the skin shows significantly more trauma than the lower levels. That could only mean that the blade came from inside out."

"Okay," Gideon responded, "so he sticks her on one side and leaves the blade in, slicing all the way across and out, right? Doc, I've seen my share of horror movies, and I gotta tell ya that every time someone gets cut like that, all their guts just come pouring out. Why was she still pretty much intact?"

Jernigan rolled her eyes. "First of all, young Jedi, a horror movie without plenty of gore kinda defeats the purpose, wouldn't ya say?"

"*Star Wars* reference," Gideon quipped, "nice . . . I didn't think ya had it in ya."

Jernigan flipped the face shield up and glared at him for a moment, and Gideon put his palms up, lowering his head.

"Sorry," he said, "please continue . . . Yoda."

"Cute . . . asshole. You know, I do actually have a life outside of this basement!"

"I said I was sorry. Go on, please," he said trying to contain the inevitable grin.

"As I was saying, the cut was not that deep . . . and the control-top panty hose helped a lot as well."

"Panty hose, huh?" he said, smiling.

"Yeah, well there's that," she scoffed.

"So if the cut's not that bad, then how'd she die?"

"Oh, I didn't say the cut wasn't bad. I said it wasn't that deep. The abdomen is a nasty place to get wounded, all kinds of vital stuff in there to mess with. Even at that depth, she's got several lacerations to her intestines in a lot of different places along the way. Even if this happened in the parking lot of this hospital, I don't know that we would have been able to control all the bleeding in time, not to mention the peritonitis. It's a nasty and painful way to go, Gideon. Not to mention, slow."

"So she got to watch him finish her off just like Lindsay Diaz?"

"Probably, she was most likely alive, but I don't know about conscious. The shock was probably enough to knock her out through most of it."

He'd hoped that he was wrong, but the theory had been nagging at him the whole time. This guy wasn't just killing people—he was making *them* watch *him* kill.

"Oh," Jernigan said, breaking his thought, "and he's left-handed too."

"And we know this how?"

"Well, the bruising around the throat was premortem. Pretty deep singular hematoma on the right side of her larynx . . . looks like a thumbprint actually. That means he grabbed her with his right hand. Plus the ventral incision right to left corroborates a left-handed killer."

"Okay great. I've got an extremely strong left-handed psycho that likes to have his victims watch while he kills them. My day just keeps getting better! What about the weapon . . . any idea?"

"I'd say that by the depth and the wound pattern on the abdomen that you're looking for something like a utility knife."

"Or a scalpel?"

"Sure," she said. "A scalpel would also work. The carving on the forehead would back that up. A thin blade, and very sharp anyway. Why a scalpel? You still thinking there's a medical angle here?"

"Well, no pun intended, but the surgical sutures from Lindsay Diaz kinda ties it together, don't ya think? And I'm having a hard time believing in coincidences anymore."

Gideon heard the footsteps outside in the hall as the door nudged open a bit with no one visible.

"Mattie, that you?" Laura yelled.

"Y-Y-Yes, Dr. Jernigan. I'm sorry I was late, but my mother was quite ill last night," the voice muttered from behind the door.

"That's okay, Mattie," she replied.

"If you would allow me, let me hang up my coat and run to the little boys' room, and I'll be in there in a jiff."

"Take your time, Mattie," she said as the door eased closed and the footsteps disappeared back down the hall. "He's such a sweet man."

"Whatever," Gideon chided. "He kinda gives me the creeps."

"Gideon, be nice. Not everyone can be a superhero, ya know."

"Anyway," he said, trying get off the topic, "I'm gonna have the lab boys come over and see if they can lift that thumbprint. Let me know when you're done, okay?"

"You got it," she said, turning back to the table.

Gideon pulled open the door and dropped the mask into the bright red biohazard bag that hung on the adjacent counter. As he stepped out into the hallway, the phone buzzed in his pocket, and he dug it out and flipped it open without looking.

"Kane?" he said, grabbing the coat off the rack and holding the phone with his cheek against his shoulder.

"Gideon . . . why are there a thousand cops outside my office?"

"Elizabeth?"

"Yeah, it's me. What's going on out here?"

"Well, honey, there was a bit of a . . . an incident last night."

"What kind of incident? Is there something I should worry about?"

"It's actually kind of complicated . . . How's your day look? I'll explain it over lunch. My treat. Whaddya say?"

"All right, lunch then. I've got to be in court at one. How about eleven thirty at Po' Boys? Then I can just walk over to the courthouse."

"Sounds good. I'll see you then."

He flipped the phone shut and hopped into the elevator as the doors closed behind him. *It's a start*, he thought. As the elevator rose, the phone buzzed again.

"Kane."

"Hey, Gideon, it's Eddie."

"Hey, bud, what's going on?"

"Everyone's headed back to the office to kinda go over everything we've got so far. You in?"

"Sounds like a plan. I'm leaving the morgue now. See you in a bit."

As he walked out onto the uncovered upper deck of the parking garage, Gideon saw the sun peeking out as the rain had all but vanished, the steam beginning to rise up from the concrete floor. As he got to the car, he quickly pulled off his coat, popped the trunk with the remote, and tossed it inside, his mind still preoccupied with her phone call.

Baby steps, he thought.

25

Gideon pressed through the door of the VCU as Eddie and Trey were both busy chatting away on the phone. Judging by the expression on their faces, Gideon surmised that Trey's call was business and Eddie's was pleasure. Jason, true to form, sat hunched over and expressionless before his computer staring blankly at his ever improving Myspace page.

"Ya know what happens when I google myself?" he said, still motionless as Gideon walked past.

Gideon sunk heavily into his chair and propped his feet up. "I'm so afraid to ask, you have no idea."

"Three pages, Sarge . . . three whole pages of Jason Ryden. There's a lot of *me* out there, ya know?"

Gideon laughed. "No, Jason . . . there's nobody else like you out there, trust me."

"Of course," Ryden continued, still expressionless, "it's still not as much the amount of Powell that's out there."

Still smiling, Gideon replied, "Jason, he's gonna snap you in half one day if you don't stop giving him shit about his weight."

"Yeah, I know, but I can't help it. He's like a big teddy bear, with a gun in one paw and a cheeseburger in the other. He's not gonna make retirement if he keeps eating all that crap."

Ryden stood, finally, a wide superhero grin suffused his face as he looked upward. "As God is my witness . . . I will get him to eat a salad one day!"

Gideon's head fell forward to his chest as he shook his head chuckling. He wondered to himself how this motley group of mostly cynical malcontents was ever gonna catch anyone at anything, and it made him chuckle more.

Trey screamed into the phone, "Oh yeah . . . thanks a lot, pal! Fine! I'll see you then!" He slammed down the phone.

Gideon looked up, cocking his head, staring through one open eye as both Ryden and Eddie broke from their own little worlds to check out the crazy guy.

"What?" Trey asked, his voice still elevated.

"What the hell was that?" Gideon asked.

"Uhh . . . you and I have an appointment with Stiles again in an hour."

"Great, anything on the video?"

"He says the system was working," Trey said, "but it's not digital. It's an old VHS system, and they just rewind the tape at the end of the cycle, so the image may be pretty degraded. He said we can look at it when we get there."

"He hasn't looked at it yet?"

Gritting his teeth, Trey continued, "Well, see there's why I'm a little edgy on this one. It seems that the duke of Dewey decimals has, predictably, locked himself out of his office. I imagine it's gonna be a bit before we get in there!"

Gideon smiled as he closed his one open eye again. It was all he could think to do as Trey explained to Eddie and Jason the tribulations of the keymaster. Although *Ghostbusters* seemed to be just about Jason's speed, he was completely lost about the keymaster reference until Eddie smacked him on the back of the head and proceeded to explain in incessant detail the brilliance that is Bill Murray. After a couple more smacks and locker room repartee, a welcome silence finally swept across the room, and Gideon could concentrate on the pulsing of the impending migraine.

"Anyone know where Powell is?" Gideon asked, his eyes still closed.

Jason stood up quickly, not so much because he knew the answer, but because Eddie had managed to strike the exact same spot with each successive blow, and it was beginning to hurt.

"I think he's still down in the records room trying to track down the Abigail Arbin thing," Ryden said while wincing and rubbing the back of his head.

"All right," Gideon said, "until he gets here, let's gather 'round and see how close we are to catching this son of a bitch. Eddie, you can spank Jason later."

"Thanks, boss," Eddie said, a devious smile overcoming him as he turned to Ryden.

Eddie continued, "Okay . . . preliminary lab results say that the fingerprints recovered off of both bodies belong to the same guy."

"Yeah, we needed *them* to tell us that," Trey mocked.

"We've put it into AFIS," Eddie continued, "but there's no match yet."

Gideon rubbed his brow. "Great, so we're looking for a ghost."

"Yeah, something like that," Eddie replied, "but new bad guys get added to the system every day though, so maybe we'll get a hit soon."

Flustered, Gideon threw his arms in the air. "Problem is, fellas, we don't have soon to wait. What else we got?"

The four of them began tossing around the various dead-end leads that they'd managed to come up with so far, trying to make some kind of sense of it, the theory being that if you threw enough shit against the wall, some of it is bound to stick. Trey related that the lab hadn't been able to exclusively identify the button they had recovered from the library—only that it was made of a low-grade, nickel-plated zinc and was standard issue on a thousand different types of jackets and coats from a thousand different designers, all of which sold their wares in the Tallahassee area.

"What about Ronnie Shaw?" Gideon posed. "He said that *he'd* been the one to suggest to Lindsay that she do the bird story at the park, right?"

"Right," Ryden jumped in, "and he also said that she had gotten the mysterious phone calls about the unsolved murder way back when."

"So where are we with that angle?" Trey asked.

Gideon stood up and began to pace frustratingly between the desks. "So she's going to the park to do the bird story anyway . . . and figures that, as long as she's there, she'll just meet the mystery man at the same place. This way, if his story doesn't pan out, she can still do the fluff piece."

"Yeah," Trey interjected, smiling. "Kill two birds with one stone . . . get it?"

Gideon stopped pacing and stared at the allegedly soothing green carpet as Eddie tried to muffle a laugh with his hand.

Jason continued, "Well, Shaw says that the guy never gave his name, and we have no way of tracking the call. He didn't seem to know her, but he asked for her specifically. Other than that, I honestly don't think he knows anything helpful."

Gideon nodded in agreement. "Right. Shaw didn't strike me as motivated enough to wipe his own ass, let alone pull off two murders this intricate."

Jason reached down into the top drawer of his desk and pulled out a clear plastic evidence bag, a small yellow square of paper visible within. "However, when Joe and I went to the television station, I got this from Lindsay's desk. I didn't know what the 'bring your glasses' thing meant until Gideon figured out the whole binocular thing."

"Doesn't tell us much except that he actually talked to Lindsay at some point," Eddie piped in.

"Hey, wait a minute," Jason said, suddenly realizing something. "I almost forgot something that the hot secretary mentioned to me. Her name was Tiffany, I think. Blond hair, awesome eyes, this tight sweater that showed off this enormous set of . . ."

"Jason!" Gideon boomed.

"Oh right, sorry. Anyway, Tiffany said that she talked to the guy a few different times in the days prior to the murder. Said that when he got angry, he began to stutter."

Trey leaned over to Gideon and whispered, "Great . . . a lunatic who stutters. That oughta narrow it down a tad." Louder now, he turned to Eddie. "I still think Nelson Diaz's hidin' something."

"That's the father, right?" Eddie asked.

"Yeah, he does have kind of a sleazy vibe about him," Gideon added. "We just don't have anything to press him on yet."

"I'll keep digging on Diaz," Trey said. "We're missing something. I just can't put my finger on it."

"Yeah," Gideon replied, "that stuttering thing is nagging at me for some reason. Not sure why yet." He continued, "Anything else?"

"Yeah," Ryden said, "I need a haircut."

"You need a lobotomy," Eddie chimed in.

Trey stood up. "Alrighty then, gentlemen, I'd say that about wraps up this episode of *We Don't Know Dick*! Gideon, we gotta motor. Stiles should have found the keys by now. Your c-c-car or mine?" he said, grinning widely.

"Cute, real cute," Gideon remarked. "Let's take both. I've got a lunch date right after."

"A date huh? With whom?" A plastic expression of surprise washed over his face. "It wouldn't be the lovely Ms. Pierce now, would it?"

"Don't worry about it," he said, moving quickly toward the door.

"It is Liz, isn't it? You lucky dog you."

Gideon pushed through the door, agitated. "It's not what you think, Trey. It's just lunch. I've gotta explain why there was a dead body in front of her office this morning, that's all."

"Baby steps, Gideon . . . baby steps."

Gideon paused at the elevator frozen, recalling the words as he looked back at Trey. He pushed the button and smiled as he glanced back at Trey. "How do you do that?"

"It's a gift, man. I do what I can. Sherrell hates it by the way . . . thinks I'm all up in her brain."

"I imagine so."

As they exited the elevator at the first floor and made their way to the parking lot, they each hopped in their cars. Trey took the lead as Gideon followed close behind. After only a moment, Gideon realized his mistake in letting Trey lead this procession. With the possible exception of the decrepit old lady who drove the short bus, Trey may have been the slowest human being with a driver's license. The majority of it stemmed from the fact that Trey loved being in his car because it afforded him the ability to avoid everyone. Like Gideon, he thought that civilization was great—except for all the people involved. Traffic was thick now, and they passed through the south end of campus at a crawl. Gideon hated doing anything slowly, and ten agonizing minutes later, they had finally arrived at the Park Avenue Library.

Stiles was pacing back and forth in the shade on the front portico at the top of the steps as they approached him.

"What are you doing out here?" Trey asked. "Please don't tell me you locked us out again."

"No, gentlemen," Stiles muttered timidly. He stopped his pacing and stared intently at the ground. "It's nothing like that at all. The cleaning people just left, and all that blood . . ." Stiles's face turned ashen. "It's just quite unsettling and all. I was just not in the mood to be in there alone any longer, that's all. I just needed some fresh air for a moment."

"Mr. Stiles, we really would like to get a look at those tapes as soon as possible," Gideon prodded.

"Of course, of course, gentlemen. Please follow me, I believe I'm feeling much better now."

Stiles turned and pulled open the door, stepping gingerly inside as Trey and Gideon followed him through.

Trey leaned over to Gideon, cupping his hand near his mouth. "He's better now?" he whispered, "Hate to see what he looked like before we got here."

They made their way behind the main desk and down the adjacent hallway past Stephanie's open door, the smell of bleach and antiseptic wafting all around them.

"Right through here, gentlemen," Stiles said.

SEE NO EVIL (THE GIDEON KANE FILES)

Stiles's office was just a few feet further down the hall, and the surveillance system's access terminal was located in an unassuming Sauder Bradford credenza stuffed into a corner.

"I've isolated the monitor on the camera covering the alley door," Stiles said, motioning them both to sit. "I assumed that would be most helpful to you. I didn't have the stomach to watch it myself . . . you understand. I'll take my leave of you now, if you don't mind, while you conduct your investigation. I believe you should have no problem operating the system. It's merely a standard video-cassette recorder. Should you need me, I shall be just outside at the main desk."

Stiles turned and began to walk out as Gideon called to him.

"Uh, Herman, one more thing. I understand that you keep detailed records of your clientele and their respective literary habits, is that true?"

"We keep impeccable records here, Detective Kane. What exactly might you be looking for?"

"Well," Gideon pulled a slip of paper from his pocket and handed it to Stiles, "I was wondering if you could tell me who has checked out that book. Say . . . in the last few months."

"Ahh," Stiles gasped. "It is a clue, is it?"

"More of a hunch, Mr. Stiles."

"I believe we can oblige you with that, Detective. I won't be but a few minutes. Please make yourselves at home in my absence."

Stiles disappeared through the doorway as Gideon turned back toward the monitor. Trey had already begun scanning the tape.

"Tell me you don't wanna just snap his neck like a twig," Trey offered, still staring intently at the screen.

"He's a little grating, I'll give you that."

A blur moved across the screen at three minutes before nine, and Trey quickly hit the pause button.

"What the hell was that?" Trey said.

"Can you back the camera up any? Like maybe zoom out a bit?"

"Nope. If it was digital, maybe, but this is ancient VHS. Whatcha see is whatcha get."

They played with the rewind and fast-forward for a few more minutes before they were able to isolate a figure in the hallway.

"What is that?" Gideon asked.

"It's grainy, but it looks like a guy in a long, dark coat. Looks like some kind of hat, but we're not gonna get any better detail with this piece of shit. Might as well be a cave painting."

They ran the video back and forth a few more times before finally realizing that they had all they were going to get.

"You can't even tell if it's a dude," Trey said.

"I don't know too many women that can hold someone up by the neck and do the damage that this guy's done."

"What about Roseanne Barr?"

"All right I'll give you that one . . . but she's too short."

"Right, too short," Trey said as his skin insula furrowed in deep thought. "What about Wonder Woman . . . she was an Amazon chick . . . they're tall, right?"

"Yes, Trey, they are quite tall." Gideon relented as Stiles thankfully walked back through the door.

"Herman, please tell me you have good news."

"I'm afraid not, Detective Kane."

Gideon noticed that Stiles's eyebrows were arched in a manner that conveyed he knew something others did not.

"You've got nothing?"

"Well, according to the archive database, the *Lesser Key of Solomon* hasn't been checked out since 1983."

"Nineteen eighty-three? How is that possible? I thought you kept impeccable records."

"Oh, we do, Detective, but on occasion, certain persons take it upon themselves to remove certain items from this facility without following proper checkout procedures."

"Oh, Herman, who the hell would steal a book from the library when they don't cost anything to check out?"

"Hmmm, let me see," Stiles mused, "the book does not appear to be in the stacks at this present time, and as far as I can tell, you were the last person to have possession of this particular tome . . . and yet your name does not appear on the register either."

"Oh . . . well, there's that, but I can explain . . ."

"By the way," Stiles said, his expression turning more stern, "the *Kama Sutra* is due back Friday."

"*Kama Sutra* huh?" Trey teased. "Thought it was just lunch?"

Gideon looked down at his watch. "Oh shit!"

He stood up quickly, knocking the chair backward onto the floor.

"Listen, Trey, get a copy of that tape and take it back to the office. Maybe we can get it enhanced. Stiles, I'm sorry, but I've gotta run. I'm late for a meeting . . . and I promise, I'll have the, uh, *other* book back by Friday."

Gideon ran out of the office and out into the sunlight, trying to remember where he'd parked. The restaurant was only a few blocks away.

26

As he reached the car, he knew he was late, but the realization suddenly hit him that at this time of day, he'd never get another parking space along College Avenue, and the odds were slim that he'd get one any closer than he already was. Po' Boys was a popular Creole restaurant, only one block from the county courthouse and a mere three blocks from the capitol building. In mere minutes, hundreds of young, self-absorbed yuppie lawyers, lobbyists, legislators and their aides, college students, and professors would all descend upon the downtown area in a frenzied search for sustenance. The restaurant was almost always packed, partly because of the location, but mostly just because the food was simple, quick, and amazing. Ordinarily, an outdoor hardwood deck on the corner of a busy downtown intersection might not play too well, but here, you felt like family. A laid-back atmosphere comprised of muted tones of orange on the walls, lots of old photographs tucked neatly here and there, as well as the obligatory number of plasma TVs to assure every patron an unprecedented view of every major sporting event from anywhere in the place.

Of course, you also had a moderately sized contingent of the snooty upper crust that considered eating Creole food to be chic—privileged men and women who hadn't set foot in a kitchen in years, let alone prepared their own meals, who felt that this rustic fare was once considered only suitable for the impoverished. It was their own self-aggrandizing way of connecting with the have-nots and stroking their ravenous egos into truly believing that they were in tune with the common man. Elizabeth and Gideon, on the other hand, just ate there because they liked the food. Gideon liked anything spicy, and Elizabeth had spent a few years attending school in New Orleans. As far as they were concerned, they were there for all the right reasons, and this was *their* place.

Gideon ran up the stairs to the crowded deck and quickly moved past them toward the door to the inside dining area. In this heat, he knew Elizabeth would be inside. As he walked through the glass doors, he looked left and spotted her sitting at a booth along the wall. Two unsweetened iced teas and a basket of fried pickles sat neatly in the middle as she nibbled away. Spotting him between bites, she raised her hand and waved, a curt smile disappearing before he could return the gesture.

"Hey, honey, sorry I'm late," he offered, sliding into the booth across from her. "Trey and I were over at the library going over surveillance tapes, and I just lost track."

"That's okay. I ordered for us already. Hope you don't mind. I've gotta be in court soon."

"No, that's fine," he said, grabbing one of the iced teas, taking a generous chug.

"Why're you sweating?" she asked. "What did you do, run all the way over here?"

"Uh, actually . . . yeah, I did." A boyish grin of embarrassment washed over him as she began to giggle. "I knew I was late, and I had such a good space over there, and I figured I'd just be even later if I tried to find one over here, so I ran, okay?"

"There's like three spaces right across the street," she said, smiling.

"How did I know that? Besides, you walk over here all the time. What's the difference?"

Still mocking him, she grinned. "The difference would be that I didn't run five blocks in ninety-seven-degree heat wearing a suit."

"I just didn't want you to wait, that's all. Cut me some slack. I guess I just thought you might . . ."

"Leave?"

"Yeah . . . leave."

"You know I wouldn't have done that, Gideon . . . unless you were really late, that is." They both smiled as she lifted her glass to toast.

"To us having a pleasant lunch together."

Gideon lifted his glass. "Hear, hear!"

"And to large walk-in closets!"

They both fought through a bit of nervous laughter and noshed on the pickles for a moment as the uncomfortable silence crept in. They'd never had that in the past.

"Now cut the crap, Kane," she said, still smiling. "What's with the circus outside my office? What happened?"

The smile ebbed from Gideon's face as the soiled white linen sheet flashed back in his head.

"Well, ya know that bench outside your office that you said was the one you were sitting on the last time you talked to—"

"Yeah, yeah," she said, abruptly cutting him off and not wanting to go there. "What about it?"

"We found a girl murdered early this morning on that very bench . . . I think it's cursed or something."

"Oh my God, Gideon!" she yelled, reaching across the table and slapping him on the shoulder. "You couldn't tell me that before?"

"Sorry, Liz, I just didn't think it was something to talk about over the phone."

She slid back down in her seat and collapsed against the back of the booth, a dazed look still prevalent on her face.

"How did she die?" Liz begged, a more inquisitive look coming over her.

"It was bad."

"Bad?"

"Yes, bad."

"There's a dead girl on my front doorstep, and the only adjective you can come up with is *bad*?"

"She was gutted from hip to hip," he said abruptly.

Elizabeth cupped her hand over her mouth. "I think the pickles are making a comeback."

"You see, this is why I don't tell you things."

"I'm kidding, Gideon," she replied, her pallor waning. "Do you think it's related to the other one?"

"Oh yeah, it's the same guy."

For the next few minutes, Gideon explained the intricacies of both murders while Elizabeth sat transfixed, as if listening to ghost stories as a child around the campfire. He talked about the missing eyes, the mysterious black sedan, and the enigma that was the stranger in the long black coat. He didn't want to, but he glossed quickly over some of the occult stuff hoping that maybe she'd validate him, and he'd stop feeling completely crazy for even considering it.

"So how close are you?" she asked.

"I don't know. Something's bothering me about this whole thing. We've got a lot of little stuff that, at least on the outside, doesn't seem to help a whole lot. But I think we're headed in the right direction, and I can't explain why. Something's nagging at me . . . like I'm missing something obvious, ya know?"

"Like what?"

"I don't know. Ever since this started, I get the weird feeling that I'm being watched . . . like this guy is following me or something."

"Followed? Why? How?"

"I knew this one."

"You knew her?" she said, crossing her arms.

"Yeah. I was supposed to meet her last night, and she never showed up. Then Trey calls me a few hours later, and we find her dead on your bench."

"First of all, it's not my bench, and second, what do you mean you were supposed to meet her?"

Flustered, he continued, "She worked at the library. I thought there might be a connection there, and she was gonna meet me after they closed to let me take a look at her files."

"Her files, huh? Is that what we're calling it nowadays?"

Gideon began to laugh. "Yes, files, that's all. Anyway, when she wasn't there to meet me, I started to walk over to your office to see how you were doing, and I guess I just missed you because I saw you drive away before I made it across the park."

"What time was that?" she asked.

"About nine thirty, I guess. Why?"

Her brow furrowed, a confused look forming. "Gideon . . . Max hasn't been feeling too well the past couple of days, so I went home about six."

"That wasn't your car?"

"No. If someone's following you, do I have something to be worried about?"

"No, no, no," he said in the most "Don't be ridiculous" manner he could summon.

"I went by your house after and checked on you. Don't worry about anything."

"You checked on me?" An innocent smile peeked through. "That's sweet."

Feeling the nervousness of a schoolboy caught staring across the classroom, he was quickly relieved as her phone rang.

"Elizabeth Pierce . . . Oh hi, Mom." To Gideon: "It's my mother." She said.

"I gathered that," he mocked.

"Really? Okay, try to keep them apart, and I'll be there in a minute."

"Bye, Joy!" Gideon yelled as she clicked off the phone.

"My mother says to say hi."

"Tell her hi back."

"Listen, Gideon, I'm sorry about this, but I've gotta run back to the office and take care of this before I go to court."

"But we haven't eaten yet," he pleaded.

"I know, I'm sorry, but the Langstons are in my office about to beat the crap out of each other. Can I get a rain check?"

"Sure," he conceded. "How about dinner . . . tonight, maybe?"

"Deal," she said as she stood, leaning over and giving him a hug.

"Melting Pot? Nine o'clock?"

"Sounds good," she said. "I'll see you there."

With that, he sat there watching as she disappeared through the doors and out onto the deck.

If she looks back, that's good, he thought. She didn't.

154

As she walked through the throng of people on the deck and made her way down the stairs, he looked up from under his cap, catching a fleeting glimpse of her skirt as she vanished from view.

She will be perfect for us, will she not?

"Yes . . . she shall," he whispered.

He glanced over through the doors and watched as Gideon sat motionless, staring blankly at the stairway.

Yes . . . she shall . . .

27

Gideon knew he was in a bad place. He was neck-deep in a homicide investigation that was eerily similar to a merry-go-round—there was a great deal of motion, but they didn't seem to be getting anywhere. The Dark Man, whom he'd come to refer to the killer in his own head, was most certainly going to do it again. There had been only two bodies thus far—hardly enough to qualify him as a serial killer just yet. But everyone had agreed that there must have been others that they hadn't yet been able to connect. If that was the case, killers of that ilk tended to work on schedules. Whether those schedules were dependent on the phase of the moon or a specific day of the month or even the anniversary that their favorite sitcom was cancelled, they tended to stick to their schedule.

For certain serial killers, there was also an agenda to take into consideration. While you certainly did have the Gacy's and Bundy's of the world who simply killed when their insanity meters had filled up, there were others whose violent actions were merely a means to an end. Each murder was simply a piece of their own sick and twisted cerebral puzzle that, once complete, often made sense only to them. As they neared the end of their journey through crazy land, however, things tended to speed up and schedules accelerated. Much like the rest of us when faced with a long, arduous task, as we near the end, we just want it to be over. Even if it started off as pleasurable, the monotony and repetition give way to the desire for accomplishment, completion, and, most importantly, recognition. Corners are cut, shortcuts are abused—and mistakes are made. Gideon had relegated the Dark Man to this final category.

There had been only two days between the murders, and if the acceleration theory held any credence, Gideon had very little time to stop the third. On the one hand, this was actually the easy side of the "bad place." The more difficult task lay in Elizabeth's endless parade of entries and exits into Gideon's consciousness. With the burden of solving the case squarely upon his shoulders, he didn't have the luxury of being distracted. When she left him, he had thrown himself into his work to avoid the thought of her, and it had worked for a little while, at least. But as more time passed without her around, he found himself scrounging for memories in order to get his fix. She had been his world, and all he wanted in life was to take care of her—and her face was around every corner.

I'm pathetic, he thought.

As she disappeared down the steps and out of view, the waitress approached the table and placed the dishes in front of him: the chicken wrap for her and a muffuletta for him. She remembered. That was something, at least. He stood and handed the young girl a twenty, telling her politely to keep the change and the food.

As he made his way out onto the deck, the sunlight blinded him, and he covered his eyes as he made his way down the steps and onto the street. For a moment, her words resonated, and he thought about running back to the car just to spite her. In the heat of the day, however, he just wasn't that motivated. He walked back through the park. The crime scene tape had been pulled down, and the bench, covered in blood only hours before, had been washed down. He chuckled to himself about the metaphor as his phone buzzed.

"Kane."

"Gideon, it's Powell. You're gonna love this shit, man."

"What'd you find?"

"How soon can you get back here? I think I might have found our link, and it's a doozy."

"I'm getting in the car now. Is Trey there?"

"Yeah, he's here . . . and he's doin' a whole I-told-ya-so dance around the office."

"That can't be pretty . . . I've seen him dance. Give me a few. I'll be there as soon as I can."

Gideon flipped the phone shut as he approached the car, shutting his eyes and looking upward, the warm rays of the sun washing over his face.

"God?" he said, "if you're listening . . . and *no*, it doesn't have anything to do with Liz this time . . . could you please let this actually be something useful?"

Back at the office, he walked through the door and spied Trey sitting in his chair, feet on the desk and his hands clasped behind his head, a wide grin which could only be described as "shit-eating" displayed prominently on his face.

"What, no more dancing?" Gideon said.

"I told you so, I told you so, I told you so," Trey responded. "Powell's got the smoking gun."

"All right there, Sherlock," Gideon quipped as he plopped down into his chair. "Let's hear some good news."

Powell grabbed the top file on the stack at his desk and rolled over closer to Gideon.

"Get this," he said, "remember I was telling you about the Abigail Arbin chick from the missing persons files?"

"Yeah," Gideon replied, "and they found her in the river three weeks later with her eyes missing."

"Yeah, that one. Anyway, in 1983, Ms. Abigail Arbin takes a leisurely drive down a lonely country road in her '74 Plymouth. What she doesn't realize at the time, however, is that coming the other way is a logging truck with her name on it."

Trey chimed in, "Brutal crash, Gideon."

"Yeah," Powell continued, "the log truck jackknifed just as both of them got to an old bridge. Truck tore the bridge out from under them, and Abigail's Plymouth took a header into the river. The whole bridge collapsed on top of her, and it took them a few hours to even reach the car."

"Go ahead," Trey said, "tell him what happened next."

Powell turned quickly to Trey. "I will if you'll shut up for a minute! Anyway, when they finally get down to her car, she's gone. Cops figure she either got thrown from the car before she hit the bottom, or the current just sucked her out once she got to the bottom. Either way, nobody sees her again until she pops up downriver three weeks later."

"With no eyes," Gideon said.

"Right, with no eyes. Initially, they just chalked it up to the turtles or fish, but when the medical examiner gets the body, he says they were removed before the body ever hit the water. Something about algae concentration in the wounds or something."

"So somebody fished her out and took her eyes . . . and then put her back in? Who the hell would do that?"

"He's getting to that," Trey interposed.

"There's something else, Gideon. There's also a couple of lines in the original ME report that makes mention that the condition of ol' Abigail's body wasn't consistent with her being in the water for three weeks. A body in water, which would have been pretty cold at that time, would have been pretty well-preserved, except for the wildlife chewing on her that is. It seems Ms. Arbin was in a pretty advanced state of decomposition when she washed up on shore."

"Okay," Gideon said, "so she floats downriver from the crash, then someone pulls her out, takes her eyes, for whatever reason, and then dumps her back in the river to cover it up. That about cover it?"

"Exactly," Trey said.

"Okay," Gideon continued, "maybe I'm missing something here, but how's this connect with our guy?"

Powell flipped through the pages of the file and continued, "Turns out that Abigail had one surviving relative . . . a son."

"And?"

"Mathias Arbin, born June 6, 1966."

"Four sixes huh?" Gideon said, leaning back in his chair. "Well, that's one too many, but still kinda creepy I guess. What else?"

"After Abigail's body was recovered, legal aide stepped in to help little Mathias with a lawsuit against the trucking company. They were claiming that the load on the truck wasn't properly secured, and that the driver had been working for over twenty hours without any sleep prior to the crash."

"Negligence then?" Gideon posed.

"Right," Trey said.

Powell jumped in, "Mathias stood to make millions from the trucking company. It was open-and-shut. A first year law student could have won that case."

"Lemme guess," Gideon said, "they didn't?"

"Exactly," Powell said. "The trucking company had a *serious* high-end attorney on retainer for just such a thing."

"Guess who the lawyer was, Gideon?" Trey said, smiling.

Gideon sat up, a eureka moment striking him. "Nelson fucking Diaz!"

"Abso-fucking-lutely," Powell said.

Trey clasped his hands behind his head, smile beaming. "Nelson fucking Diaz, dude! That's huge!"

"You're really proud of yourself, aren't you?" Gideon asked him.

"Oh, you have no idea."

"So who worked it for us?" Gideon asked.

"Buck Blackstock," Powell answered.

"Wasn't he your training officer, Trey?"

"Yeah, he was. He retired a couple of years ago."

"Get up with him. See if he can shed any light on this."

"I can do that," Trey said.

"This is just starting to get interesting, gentlemen . . ."

28

Twenty-five years had passed since the trial. A simple tort case—a rather large favor for an old friend. The trucking company stood to lose millions from the accident: millions that, at the time, it did not have to spare. Sam Tate had built SJP from the ground up, starting with one old and extremely well-traveled Kenworth cab and a home-made log trailer that he'd welded together from scraps. He'd driven the first rig himself night and day, six and seven days a week just to get by in the beginning. In those days, the loads he hauled for the first three days of the week simply paid for the fuel. His diligence, however, had eventually paid big dividends. In just five short years he'd become one of, if not *the most* predominantly used shipping company east of the Appalachian Mountains. From that single used truck, SJP had grown to a fleet of more than two hundred top-of-the-line trailers, hauling millions of tons of manufacturing timber to twenty-two states. Today's fleet now had its own maintenance and supply yards dotted across the eastern seaboard, as well as a workforce of over eleven hundred dedicated employees.

It almost, however, had never happened. On a lazy summer Sunday morning in 1983, just three weeks before Sam Tate was to take SJP public, a thirty-eight-year-old matronly widow nearly brought down the world that Sam Tate had spent the last five years carving out of nothing—because she was out of bleach. Tate had first met young Abigail some ten years prior to the incident. At the time, a small town held no secrets, and no one was a stranger to the rest. As far as he was concerned, she was nothing but a pathetic and lonely little whore—desperate for attention, an embarrassment to the community. Of course, that hadn't stopped Sam Tate from making himself available, from time to time, to the many salacious talents of young Abigail Arbin. Sam had been what would be termed today as a bit of a "player." When he wasn't driving, he was availing himself of several of the town's nubile amenities, including a young coed by the name of Deborah Finch. He'd even shouted out her name once while in the throes with Abigail, causing a bit of a scene in which she chased him from the house with a rather large knife as he ran naked down the long gravel road laughing hysterically. Mathias, too, had been well-acquainted with Sam, albeit more than he cared to be. There had been many an afternoon that he had arrived home from school, only to be greeted by the lascivious cries and unmistakable grunts of his mother and the upstanding Mr. Tate reverberating down from the upstairs bedroom.

Sam had been at home that morning preparing for yet another unannounced early morning visit with Abigail to discuss their recent misunderstanding regarding the young Ms. Finch when he received the call from the driver of the rig. He was speaking loudly and quite fast as he explained that he knew he wasn't supposed to be driving on the back roads and that he had only been taking the shortcut because he was running late. He never saw the other car coming toward him because he was tired, and he felt the trailer gave way just as he approached the bridge. He knew he didn't have enough straps on the timber, but it would have taken another hour to lock it down properly. He said he was sorry for doing this, but he just didn't want to lose his job because he had a family to feed.

Sam remembered dropping the telephone in disbelief as he felt his world unraveling from this one frantic phone call. After a moment of panicked reflection, he calmly reached down, picked up the phone from the floor, and told the driver to keep his mouth shut and to tell the cops nothing that he had just mentioned. Sam was sending him help—and everything would be okay. With that, Sam Tate pressed down the switch hook, released it, and began dialing the number which would set in motion a series of events that would eventually come to pass twenty-five years later.

Nelson Diaz had been a young and fairly inexperienced prosecutor in Tallahassee and two short years removed from graduating law school at the University of Nevada, Las Vegas. This was in some ways ironic considering that Nelson Diaz never gambled in the courtroom, on the contrary, he would invariably make every conceivable effort to ensure that the deck was stacked in his favor, often resulting in an inordinate amount of plea bargaining to facilitate a guilty verdict. It didn't take long for Nelson, as well as his fellow prosecutors, that he cared only about winning at any cost and that he simply did not care to let matters of ethical ambiguity stand in his way. At the end of his second year with the State Attorney's Office, he'd also made the realization that whoever had made the statement that money was the root of all evil, had clearly never had any.

With that, he ventured out on his own, establishing a modest defense practice in a small building he'd bought for cheap, just down the street from the courthouse. Years later, he would turn that building, again, into a tidy profit as developers earmarked the old building for destruction in order to construct a series of yuppie condos. As his practice grew, the money was significantly better than the meager subsistence that civil service had provided, and he'd tasted blood. His true calling, however, became apparent that Sunday morning when he received an unexpected phone call from an old high school friend named Sam Tate.

Sam spent the first four minutes explaining each little nugget of potential liability that SJP would soon be on the hook for: including the unsecured load, the failing brakes, the overtired driver, and the traveling of a road not designated for commercial trucking. He spent the next two minutes explaining that SJP had been slated to become a publicly traded company in the next few weeks, and a substantial financial windfall could hang in the balance—a financial windfall that he would most appreciatively share with Nelson. Most importantly, however, he was six minutes in, and not a word about Abigail.

"Was anyone hurt?" Nelson asked deliberately.

"Well yeah," Sam said nervously. "Yeah there's a problem there. Seems there was a woman coming the other way on the bridge when the truck slid. She's uh . . . actually they're pretty sure she's dead."

"What do you mean 'pretty sure'? You're either dead or you're not, Sam. Which is it?"

"My driver says they haven't been able to find her yet, what with the logs and the whole bridge on top of her and everything."

"Wonderful, Sam," Diaz spoke dispassionately. "Who was it?"

"She was a nobody. A local whore, that's all . . . name was Abigail Arbin."

"Does she, I mean, *did* she have any money . . . family, anybody capable of coming after you or the company?"

"No, not really," Sam answered, sounding almost resigned. "I mean she's got a son, I think. Kind of a retard though. He's probably about eighteen or so."

"Okay, Sam, here's what you're going to do," Diaz said with a tone more exacting. "You will talk to no one about this from this point forward. You refer all questions regarding this tragic occurrence to me as *you* are too busy grieving and ensuring that the young lad, who has now been deprived of the love of his dear mother, is receiving every possible consideration from the good, honest folks of SJP, in hopes that is able to make it through this most dreadful of *accidental* developments. Got it?"

Feeling somewhat defeated, Sam muttered into the receiver, "Yeah, Nelson . . . whatever you say."

From that moment on, Nelson Diaz began stacking the deck. Having been a prosecutor, Nelson still had some favors owed to him, and he still held a tremendous amount of sway over certain people who would be able to assist him in "cleansing" the potential case against SJP. The illegal use of the back road was easily managed by the careful—albeit unfortunate for Abigail—placement of a detour sign by an unidentified member of the Department of Transportation whom Nelson had represented most advantageously in a divorce proceeding the year prior. By the time that Abigail's body had been located three weeks later, load straps had mysteriously been located under the bridge debris, indicating that it had more likely than not been the result of faulty straps and that SJP had done everything in its power to ensure the safety of the motoring public. Brake pads had been enigmatically regenerated on the wreckage of the rig that had been pulled from the ravine three weeks prior, and now currently sat in an impound yard owned by another former client of Nelson Diaz.

Six months later when the case went to trial, he was able to convince a group of twelve people too inept to get out of jury duty that as there could be no fault proven against his client, the unfortunate and untimely demise of Ms. Arbin most certainly must have arisen as the result of her own carelessness. He went on to explain how she had been speeding as she approached the bridge from the south, losing control and crossing over into the other lane; and how the unfortunate and heroic truck driver was not able to see her until the last moment, and valiantly attempted to maneuver his rig to avoid striking her, and in doing so, he lost control through no fault of his own. In the course of a little over three hours, Nelson Diaz successfully managed to transfer the onus of culpability for that day's series of ill-fated events squarely into the lap of one very dead Abigail Arbin. He had even gone as far as to facilitate the attachment of monies from Abigail's estate in order to pay for the replacement of the bridge and SJP's truck and trailer. Diaz left nothing to chance. In the days after the verdict clearing the company of any wrongdoing, trading of shares of SJP tripled, thanks to no one save Nelson Diaz, Esquire. In the years that followed, Nelson's reputation for ruthlessness and winning preceded him into any room he entered. He was untouchable—until now.

Mona's voice beckoned from the intercom on his desk, "Mr. Diaz, I have Sam Tate on line one for you."

Nelson sat quietly leaning back in his chair, staring blankly across the room at the portrait hung adjacent to the door. It was of him and Lindsay around the time of her tenth birthday. She had paid out of her own allowance, which was considerably more than that received by her peers, to have it painted from photographs she'd managed to swipe from her mother's photo album. She'd given it to him on her tenth birthday as sort of a reverse thank-you-for-having-me gesture. It had been the only time he could ever recall crying.

Nelson leaned forward grudgingly and pressed the speaker button before leaning back again.

"Nelson, old friend, how are you this glorious morning?"

"Cut the crap, Sam!" he snapped. "You know why I'm calling!"

"You wouldn't be recording this now, would you, Nelson? Because as I'm sure you're aware, that would be quite illegal."

"No I'm not recording anything, you asshole! It's him . . . I know it's him!"

"Nelson, you're being ridiculous. That was twenty-five years ago. Why now?"

Nelson's voice cracked as the moisture left his throat, "Because they found my baby the same way . . ."

"The same way as what, you sniveling bitch? That Arbin woman? You can't be serious, Nelson! That was the fish, or even snakes that did that to her or something."

"My baby girl had her eyes removed, you prick! Do you have any idea how that feels! To know you're responsible for that sick shit, you pretentious son of a bitch! I never should have done it . . . *we* shouldn't have done it!"

"Hey listen, Nelson, don't you go getting any crazy ideas now about absolving your sins or some shit! You're as complicit as I am!"

Nelson said, his voice defeated, "Everything I've done . . . everything I've become . . . everyone I've destroyed, for what? The one pure thing I've done in my life . . . the one unselfish thing . . . gone."

"Listen, Nelson, whatever you need me to do all right, you just ask. But for the love of God, keep your mouth shut! It's not going to bring her back."

"No more, Sam . . . no more . . ."

The unmistakable sound resonated through the speakerphone as Sam Tate called his name over and over without response. In one motion, he'd pulled the old stainless Colt revolver from the top desk drawer, placed the barrel in his mouth, and without hesitating even for a moment—he pulled the trigger. The .45 caliber hollow point bullet removed most of the rear of Nelson's skull, depositing it not so neatly on the bookshelves behind him. Mona began screaming long before she reached him and continued as she burst through the door. Nelson Diaz was now leaning back in his leather chair, eyes open, arms at his side. As the muscles in his lifeless body eased into release, a small silver charm with a single word engraved on it fell from his hand, landing on the floor as the blood pooled up around it: *Lindsay*.

29

Trey rolled the chair back over to his desk and began flipping through the Rolodex for Buck Blackstock's phone number. Gideon grabbed the Arbin file from Powell. The majority of the paperwork inside was traffic reports from the highway patrol including photographs of the crash scene and handwritten diagrams with lots of coefficients of friction and notes on the Locard exchange principle, which was just a fancy way of telling you that when two things crashed into each other, things were gonna rub off from one item to the other. As he flipped to the narrative portion of the trooper's report, though, Gideon found several pages that appeared to have been scratched out, as though the writer had changed his mind. The old carbon paper had smeared and faded in the years since, but it looked like the condition of the timber truck had been altered at some point. It would be impossible to decipher exactly what had gone wrong in the crash from these old files. But a real live witness—now there was something that Gideon could work with.

Buck Blackstock had been an old-fashioned deputy sheriff for almost thirty years, and by all accounts, a pretty damn good one known as much for his integrity as he was for having very little patience for the stupid in people. Buck learned the trade in the days before video cameras and public information officers and victim advocates—a time when the justice system was geared more toward an "eye for an eye" than today's politically correct slant toward reha- bilitation. Toward the end of his career, Buck had a harder and harder time dealing with one too many bad guys walking on technicalities and the agency's move toward a kinder, gentler brand of law enforcement. Kissing ass was definitely not Buck's forte, and in the end, it had ultimately forced him to make the decision to leave the work that he lived for.

Trey dropped the phone back into the cradle. "Buck's on his way over, Gideon. Says he remembers the Arbin thing like it was yesterday."

"Does he remember anything good, that's the question," Gideon muttered, still peering down intently at the smeared carbon.

"Says he remembers enough to put someone in jail . . . that good enough for ya?"

Ryden clicked the hold button on his phone as he turned quickly toward Gideon. "Uhh, boss? I think you're gonna want to pick up line two."

"What now, Jason? Lemme guess . . . Myspace wants to talk to me about the questionable material on your personal page."

"Not exactly, Gideon. Nelson Diaz just blew his fucking head off in his office."

Gideon looked up with not so much genuine surprise.

"Woo-hoo!" Trey screamed as he launched out of his chair. "I told you that son of a bitch was hiding something!"

"When did this happen?" Gideon asked, looking back over at Ryden.

"Just a few minutes ago. Secretary heard a loud pop come from inside his office and found him prone out in a chair. Patrol units down there now said half his head's gone."

"As my youngest son would say . . . *awesome!*" Trey yelled.

Gideon shook his head and rubbed the bridge of his nose as the headache began to manifest.

"I guess it always turned me on when someone dies like that," Trey ranted. "I got this one, Gideon. You stay here and wait for Buck."

With that, Trey scrambled out the door like a kid barreling down the stairs on Christmas morning in search of the inevitable bounty.

"There's something seriously wrong with that dude," Ryden said.

"You ain't telling me anything I don't already know, Jason."

Gideon continued to look through the photographs in the file. From the look of Abigail's powder blue Plymouth, it was probably a good thing she was ejected before the bridge collapsed on top of it. After twenty minutes of innocuous Polaroids, Buck Blackstock pushed through the office door, and Gideon was sure he'd glimpsed a bit of a smile on the old man's face.

"Good to be back, old man?" Gideon taunted.

"Hell, no," Buck grunted. "I see ya'll still can't do shit without me, huh?"

Gideon stood and smiled. "Wouldn't have it any other way, Buck," he replied, motioning for him to sit.

"So what are ya'll digging into with the Arbin woman anyway?" Buck was not one for pleasantries.

"Well," Gideon replied, handing him the file, "we've had two pretty fucked up murders in the last few days, and Powell seems to think that there's a possibility they're related to your traffic crash twenty-five years ago. Neat, huh?"

"How the hell ya'll figure that?"

Gideon continued, "It looks, at least, like the condition of Abigail's body matches the MO for the homicides we're working."

"Yours missing the eyes too?"

"Absolutely."

Buck leaned back in the chair, tossing the file on Gideon's desk and sighed heavily. "I always thought there was something strange with that boy," he mumbled.

Gideon leaned forward. "What boy?" he asked.

"It's always bothered me, Gideon, but I never had enough to do anything with it, ya know?"

"Enough with what?"

"Well, that day, after the crash, I go to the Arbin house to make the death notification, right?"

"Yeah, but you hadn't found the body yet, right?"

"Yeah but . . . well you saw the photos. There was no way anyone coulda survived that. We didn't play around with being sympathetic back then. She was dead!"

"Fair enough," Gideon relented.

"Anyway, so when I get there, I'm banging on the door for five minutes. I can see her boy Mathias standing there in the hallway staring at me. The whole time I'm lookin' at him and calling to him and he's just not moving. He's just standing there staring at a spot on the carpet and staring up at me back and forth, back and forth . . . it was weird."

"So what's his problem?"

"After a while, he finally comes to the door and opens it. He's got this look on his face like I'd just figured out everything he'd ever done wrong in his life, right? I go into the whole 'I'm sorry for your loss' speech, and when I'm done . . . he lets out this sigh . . . like he's relieved or something."

Gideon leaned back in thought. "What can you tell me about the crash, Buck?"

"Whaddya want to know?"

"Well, the file seems to make the whole thing Abigail's fault. Is that the way it went down?"

Buck chuckled and leaned back in the chair, his hands interlaced on his stomach. "Hell no, son. She didn't have no more to do with that accident than you did with the Kennedy assassination."

"But the trooper's report says that everything about the truck was kosher. Says that she was speeding and went into the other lane . . . made the truck veer off and hit the bridge?"

"Gideon, look at the pictures! If she'd have made it that far across the bridge, her car woulda landed on the other side."

"So what happened then?"

"That road, or bridge for that matter, wasn't designed for trucks like that. That guy shouldn't have been there in the first place."

"Whaddya mean?"

"Listen, I had worked that area for eight years back then. I know that the troopers said there was a road sign saying it was okay for commercial trucks to use that bridge . . . but I'm tellin' ya . . . there was never no sign there before!"

Buck stood up and slowly walked over to the window, staring out over the city.

Gideon opened the file again and flipped through to the inventory of the truck.

"What can you tell me about the truck?"

"I can tell you that *that* truck had way too much timber on it for the size of its trailer, and it wasn't cinched down right either."

Gideon looked up from the file confused. "But according to the report, the truck had all the required straps and chains it was supposed to have."

Buck spun around. "I don't give a good goddamn what that report says. I saw two straps on that truck!" he snapped. "That truck was hauling sixty tons of timber! Do you honestly think that two piddly ol' straps were gonna hold that much weight, son?"

Gideon pondered the thought for a moment. "Well, there's that I suppose."

"All right then," Gideon continued, "what about her body?"

"What about it? We just figured she got thrown from the car and carried downriver. I only put her in the missing persons computer in case somebody happened to come across what was left. At the least the kid would have had something to bury."

"The eyes, Buck . . . the eyes?" Gideon pleaded.

"Well, that was just plain fucked up that was. The brass' tryin' to tell me that the fish had eaten 'em or something. That's bullshit, and they knew it. Gideon, you've seen bodies left in water for a long time . . . you know what fish do."

"Yeah, they nibble away at the soft tissue . . . ears . . . eyelids . . ."

"Right, but there wasn't any of that. It was like someone went in and scooped out the eyes on purpose. Who the hell would do that?"

"I'm right there with ya, Buck. Listen, thanks for coming down. If we need anything else, I'll give you a call. Save you a trip."

"That's okay, Gideon. It feels kinda good to be back in it for a little bit, ya know?"

They shook each other's hands as Buck ambled toward the door, taking it all in one last time as he disappeared into the hallway.

"That guy's a trip, Gideon," Jason remarked.

Gideon stared out the window as Buck had done earlier. "Yeah, Jason . . . but I trust him, and in this business, that's rare. Why don't you go pay a visit to this Mathias Arbin guy. See if maybe there's anything to Buck's hunch."

"I'm on it," he said as he bolted out the door.

Looking out the window over the people down below, Gideon whispered, "Where are you?"

30

Ryden eased along the gravel road and spotted the house set off the road near a small bend as he pulled into the driveway. The old white clapboard was fading, but it was an old house. He figured at some point it was probably considered a grand old mansion.

The driveway was empty and pulled all the way up to the garage door. He noted that it was made of aluminum and appeared to have been an add-on at some point. He exited the car and began walking up the faded red brick walkway up to the porch. A large sturdy wooden door inlaid with expensive beveled glass greeted him. He grabbed the brass knocker and banged it a few times, pacing around for a bit with no answer. He stepped back off the porch and peered up at the second-story windows, thinking maybe someone was upstairs and didn't hear the door.

"Hello?" he yelled without a response.

Ryden walked back toward the driveway and past as he turned around the side of the house and continued toward the backyard. He looked around and saw the rear door at the top of two steps, a pair of large Wolverine boots baking in the afternoon sun. An odd noise caught him from behind as he turned toward the large wooden shed to his right. Curious, he moved slowly toward it, the rustling sound growing louder as he approached.

"Hello? Anyone in there? Sheriff's office . . . I just want to ask you a few questions."

Jason reached down and grabbed the handle on the shed door and pulled slightly as he snuck a peek into the dark space through the crack.

"Can I help you, sir?" The voice caught him by surprise from behind and spun him around as he let go of the handle, the door sliding back closed.

"I'm sorry. I didn't see you standing there. Are you, Mathias Arbin?"

"Why yes," he answered softly, "and you would be . . . ?"

"Oh. I'm sorry. I'm Detective Ryden with the sheriff's office. I'd like to ask you a few questions about your mother, if you don't mind."

"Mother?" he answered. "Whatever for?"

"Well, sir, I understand she was killed in a car accident several years back."

"Twenty-five to be exact . . . and it was hardly an accident. But please continue."

"Well, that's what I have some questions about, Mr. Arbin, can you tell me anything about it?"

"What is there to say? Mother was on her way to the store. After a while, she did not return, and then one of your deputies came to tell me she had been taken from me."

"Yes, sir, that much we know. I understand there was a civil trial after that?"

"Ahh yes . . . the circus as it were. First my dear mother is taken from me, and then I am forced to endure a travesty of epic proportions only to be told that my mother was responsible for her own death . . . absolutely absurd."

"And why do you say that?"

"My mother was an excellent driver. She would never have done the things they accused her of. The fact of the matter is that owners of the trucking company were at fault, but were able to buy their way out any culpability whatsoever."

"So you were upset about the verdict?"

"Of course, young man!" Mathias said giggling. "But unfortunately, it happens every day in America. The rich have the means to escape their just punishments. That is simply the way it is."

"What about your mother's body? Didn't her . . . condition concern you in any way?"

"Her condition? She had been missing for three weeks when they found her washed up on the banks downriver from here. What kind of condition might she have been in?"

"I was more concerned about her eyes, Mr. Arbin . . . that they had been removed?"

"Ahh yes . . . the eyes. They did not let me see her then, God rest her soul, but I was told that the creatures of the deep had been responsible for her final repose. Was that not the case?"

"We're not exactly sure, sir. That's why I'm asking."

Mathias looked down at his wristwatch and back up at Ryden. "I'm sorry, Detective. I would like to be more help to you, but I have a pressing dinner engagement shortly. I'm meeting two old friends to discuss some other business matters. Perhaps you could leave me your card and we could schedule an appointment to talk further."

"That would be fine, sir," Ryden said, pulling a card from his pocket. "If you think of anything, please give me a call."

"Oh, I will, Detective. I shall be calling on you soon. Good day then."

Mathias turned and disappeared into the house as the back door creaked to a close.

Jason stood there for a moment wondering what had just happened as the phone buzzed in his pocket.

"Jason, it's Powell. You talk to Arbin yet?"

Slightly confused, Jason began walking back toward the car. "Yeah, as a matter of fact, I just finished. He's a little weird, couldn't get a fix on him . . . but he did give me the creeps. Didn't really find anything out though. Said he had a big dinner date or something, and that he'd get up with me tomorrow."

"Did you call Gideon yet?"

"No, not yet. I'll tell him tomorrow. There's no sense in working him up right now. Trey told me he's having dinner with Elizabeth tonight. Why ruin his night, right?"

"Yeah, I suppose," Powell agreed. "Just make sure to fill him in first thing in the morning."

"Not to worry, buddy. I'm all over this one."

31

Gideon pulled slowly and deliberately into the parking lot. He was early for once. As he came to a stop, he took a deep breath, his hands sweaty, still clutching the steering wheel in a death grip. He was undeniably nervous. He knew the "why" part of it, but it didn't make him any more accepting of the feeling. Truth was that Gideon was rarely nervous about anything—except when he was around *her*. That had been the good part of what had drawn them together in the first place: that teenage feeling of uncertainty and possibilities that someone gets in the pit of their stomach when they are truly preoccupied with another. He'd rationalized, correctly, that once the courtship had waned, that same nervousness that had been so enjoyable in the beginning had somehow transformed into an irrational fear of ever impending doom—a fear that one day he would wake up and she would simply be gone. Gideon couldn't help but laugh at how prophetic he had actually been.

Still clutching the wheel, he stared out across the parking lot and saw Elizabeth's car a few spots down. *She'd beat him there again*, he thought. He wiped the clamminess from his hands on his pants, took another deep breath, and stepped from the car, staring up at the heavy wooden door at the top of the steps.

The Melting Pot was a quiet and quaint little fondue restaurant on the north side of town. It had never really been a favorite of either of them, but it was the place he had picked to take her on their very first date. It had the longstanding reputation as one of the city's most romantic places to dine, and on that first date, Gideon figured he was going to need all the help he could get, considering that he could hardly breathe in the hours leading up to fateful Friday night. He was fashionably late as he arrived at her house to pick her up, having spent the previous hour and a half cleaning and disinfecting his truck so that she would be impressed. It hadn't been that clean since. He brought two roses for her, figuring a dozen would be too forward for the first date, and if all went well, there would be time for more later.

In the many hours that they had spent talking on the phone before that night, he'd become well-acquainted with her undying affection for her two Westies, Max and Oscar. Along with the flowers, he'd also brought two rawhide dog bones, red ribbons tied around each. Gideon hoped that it would show her that he had actually been listening to her when she spoke, a trait lost on most men, but direly important to the women they pursued. As she invited him in for a moment, the movie *Young Frankenstein* had been showing on the television. She offered him a glass of a 1999 Louis Jadot Pinot Noir, which he recalled inhaling due to his nerves as she talked on and on about how she loved any movie that had Madeline Kahn in it. Gideon figured that it was right about then that he saw she had a lighter laid-back side and realized that this girl might actually be a keeper. A few more bottles of wine and a couple of trays of melted cheese later—he was absolutely positive of it.

And after all this time, here he was again—yet another balmy Friday night with the rain drizzling, right back where it all began. He hoped to himself that those tiny bubbling cauldrons of melted cheese still had one more bit of magic in them.

The lights were very low as he stepped inside and saw her standing over by the bar. She was people-watching with a smirk on her face that was still unmistakable across the dimly lit room. People-watching had become something of a pastime to both of them over the years whenever they were out together. They were both constantly amused at the unending tragic comedy that was regular people out of their regular environment. As he walked over, she flashed a pleasant smile.

"On time I see," she said, glancing down at her wrist. "What's the occasion?"

"Oh nothing," he said glibly, "I'm meeting this hot chick here in a little bit. You should probably go before she gets here. She can be a tad on the jealous side sometimes, ya know?"

"Really? She sounds like a tight ass to me."

"Well, there *is* that, I guess."

"Listen," she said not missing a beat, "she probably won't show anyway, so why don't you ditch her and have dinner with me?"

"You really think she won't show?"

"Positive."

After a moment—"Ya know, you're probably right. She has been kind of mean lately."

"Hey watch it there, pal," she playfully said.

"Maybe it wouldn't hurt for us to have a drink or something."

Silent for a moment, they stared at each other before bursting into a muffled laughter and finding two seats at the end of the bar. Elizabeth ordered two glasses of House red, and they just sat and talked about nothing in particular. Suddenly, for the first time in a long time, Gideon wasn't nervous anymore.

"So how did court go today?"

"You'd never believe it if I told you," she said, rubbing her forehead.

"Good?"

"Not so much really," she said, taking a long sip from her glass. "You remember the hearing that I was supposed to be in court for?"

"Yeah."

"Well, that was supposed to be the final hearing on the Langston's divorce. Hell, they'd already agreed to everything! It was supposed to be in and out . . . easy stuff, right?"

"I'm guessing not."

"You would be correct, sir," she said, hoisting her glass. "I left you at the restaurant and got back to the office, right? As I walk in, they're screaming at each other, and her attorney is running around my office like a madman . . . chasing a parrot around the room!"

"A parrot?" he said, slightly confused and waiting for the punch line.

"It took a shit on my desk, Gideon!"

He began laughing and tried to cover his face with his hand, but to no avail.

"It's not funny," she cried.

"Yes . . . yes it is." He squeezed through an inerasable smile. "So why was there a parrot in your office again?"

Elizabeth suddenly got the look of a teenage schoolgirl who had just figured out the answers to tomorrow's pop quiz.

"This is the best part . . . she wants to call the bird as a witness. Claims that it had firsthand knowledge of his infidelity."

"No . . ."

"I know, right," she said, hardly believing it herself.

"So get this, the judge allows it . . . and the parrot starts yelling out the name of the girlfriend in open court!"

"That's so cool!" he yelled.

"I know, right?"

They laughed a little bit more and took sips from their glasses as they said nothing for another moment. The nervousness crept back a bit.

"So how have you been?" she asked.

"I'm okay," he said, nodding unconsciously. "Tired, but okay. This case is really messing with us."

"How's that going by the way? We didn't get to finish earlier. You were saying something about being followed?"

"I don't know, Liz. Something's just creeping me about this whole thing. I mean, this guy just kind of bursts on to the scene, ya know? It doesn't make any sense. Everything he's doing says that he's been at this for a while, but we've only got two bodies. It's like, after who knows how long, he finally wants us in on the game . . . it's weird."

"So maybe he's just bored. Maybe bringing you guys into it ups the ante . . . makes it more of thrill to him. Kind of like that very first cigarette you ever had. None of them ever tastes the same after that, and you just keep chasing that high, you know? It just becomes monotonous after a while . . . routine even."

"Yeah I suppose, but I still feel like he knows what I'm doing for some reason . . . like he's in my head, and he's always one step in front."

"You think he's a cop?"

"No . . . nothing like that. Another cop would have made a fucking mistake by now . . . too arrogant."

"You're thinking too much, Gideon. Just like always."

"What the hell is that supposed to mean?"

She looked away from him as she ran her finger around the rim of the glass. "I don't know, Gideon. You always overthink everything, looking for answers where there might not necessarily be any."

"You mean like us?"

"Yeah, Gideon"—her gaze rising back up to his—"something like that. Sometimes it just is what it is. Can't you accept that just once?"

He looked back into her eyes and froze for a moment. He wanted to tell her that *no* he couldn't accept that and that he still loved her more than life itself—that days that passed without her were simply days that passed, there was no life in them anymore; that his life had become a movie with subtitles where you were so busy reading the screen, but that you missed out on any emotion that might be smacking you right in the face.

In the end, he just said, "No . . . I can't, baby. It's not who I am. It's not who you used to be either. There's a reason for everything. It's just that most of the time, people are just too lazy or detached to ask why."

He reached over and cupped her hand in his own, his eyes staring right through her.

"Sometimes," he whispered, "there are things that are just too important to simply let slide because you don't understand why they're happening. Sometimes 'it is what it is' means that you miss out on what you were supposed to be . . . and stubborn never gets a second chance."

She stared back at him, her eyes wide as he noticed a tear welling and sliding down her cheek. He reached up and wiped it away as he felt the phone buzz in his coat pocket. After a moment more, he reached down and fished it out, flipping it open, their eyes still locked.

"Kane."

"Hey, Gideon, it's Eddie."

"Now's really not a good time, Eddie . . ."

"Well, partner, tell Liz I'm sorry . . . but I think we've got another body."

"*What?*"

"I don't know a whole lot right now, but dispatch just called me and said they got a nine-one-one call from some guy saying he'd just found a woman dead in the bathroom at Tom Brown Park."

"Okay . . . so who says it's our guy?"

Eddie paused for a second. "Gideon . . . the caller said her eyes were gone."

Gideon felt the rush of every word he'd just professed to Elizabeth blast through his head as he closed his eyes and took a deep breath again.

"I'll meet you there, and hey, Eddie . . . wait for me to go in. I've got a bad feeling here."

"You got it, bubba. I'll wait for you by the armory, and we'll go up together. I'll let the patrol units know to just stand by, okay?"

"Good enough. I'll see you in ten."

He flipped the phone shut as he grabbed her hands again in his.

"I'm sorry about everything, baby, but I've got to go. They think we've got another one."

"Go," she said, placing her hand on top of his, "go prove me wrong."

The corner of her mouth tweaked upward in a smile, and he brushed his hand along her cheek as he stood up and began to walk toward the door. After a few steps, he stopped.

If she's looking, it's good . . . he thought.

He turned back, and her eyes met his.

"Don't give up on this just yet, Liz. You believed in me once . . . *it* just might *not* be what *it* is this time, ya know?"

She said nothing, looking down at her glass as he turned and continued out the door.

As Gideon stepped out the door, the steady drizzle began to pick up slightly, and he pulled his collar up as he pulled his coat tight around him, the cheerless expression on her face still vivid as he made a break for the car.

Gideon took the shortcut over to the interstate and made his way back around to the east side, taking the exit to Capital Circle. It was a longer way to the park, but he would skirt most of the traffic and shave about fifteen minutes off the trip. As he pulled into the armory, the rain was steady now as he spotted Eddie's car and about a half dozen marked patrol units in the parking lot. A rookie patrol officer is quickly educated in the two primary tenets of being a successful cop. The first of which was simple enough—a good cop never goes hungry while on his shift. The obligatory and cliché donut references were enough testament to this. The second, and possibly the most important, is that a good cop never gets wet if he doesn't have to. Ask anyone who's ever been stopped by a cop in the rain. Invariably, there would be virtually no chance of getting a warning. True to form, the six patrol deputies sat comfortably dry in their cruisers. Gideon cinched his coat up again as he stepped out of the car and walked over to a soaking wet Eddie, smoke crept from his hand as he cupped a lit Winston. As he laughed at the sight of the water beading off his face, it occurred to him that apparently the tenets were clearly designed for nonsmokers.

"You know," Gideon said, "those things are gonna give you pneumonia one day."

"That's funny," Eddie answered expressionless, "and if I wasn't standing in the fucking rain about to stumble on another eyeless dead girl in a public toilet on a Friday night instead of being at home banging my wife . . . I might actually be laughing right now, smart-ass."

Eddie took a long final drag from the cigarette and let it drop to the ground, crushing out the cherry with his shoe.

"Why?" Gideon asked, perplexed.

"Why what?"

"It's pouring rain out here, and you still stomp out the cigarette like it might catch something on fire."

Eddie stood silent for a moment, his eyes squinting as the wheels turned. "You know something, Gideon? You see more of the weirdest shit in life than anyone I've ever known."

"Yeah, it's a curse," Gideon muttered, as he began to walk across the lot and toward the nearby hill into the park.

Eddie began to follow, motioning for the dry cops to keep up. "We gotta get you laid, man. You know that?"

"Yeah, I hear ya."

Eddie pointed up the hill, smiling. "There's a girl up there on the hill that's probably free tonight."

"That's just wrong, Eddie . . . just plain wrong."

As they approached the small concrete block building, Gideon drew his Glock from under his coat and took a position in the shadows on one side of the doorway. Eddie mirrored him on the other side and did a quick peek, shining his flashlight across the floor inside.

"I got nothing, Gideon."

"Nothing?"

Both of them had done long stints on the SWAT team together years back and had countless numbers of dynamic entries under their belts. As Gideon saw Eddie move around the wall and through the entryway, he quickly followed, taking up a position in the opposite corner. Eddie's shoulders slouched as he came to a stop, a look of frustration creeping in amongst the rain dripping down his face.

"What the fuck, Gideon? There's nothing here!"

Gideon's brow furrowed. "Is that good or not?"

Eddie turned and walked outside, gathering the uniforms around and instructed them to begin a wheel search outward from the building. Flashlights clicked on as they began moving outward and away from them. Eddie slipped back underneath the overhang in the entryway with Gideon, pulling another Winston from his pocket.

He lit the smoke and took a long pull, his head shaking. "This makes no sense, dude."

"Where did we get this info from, Eddie?"

"Listen, Gideon. All I know is that dispatch rang me up at the house and said some guy called in on nine-one-one saying there was a dead girl in this bathroom here with no eyeballs, man. That's all they told me when I called you."

"Nothing special about the guy, maybe a stutter or something?"

"Nope," he said, taking another drag. "Wait a minute . . . the dispatcher said that she could hear what she thought was a bunch of people talking in the background, and some stuff clanking around . . . like glass or something."

"A bunch of people and clanking . . . that's great. Do you see a bunch of fucking people here, *Eddie*? Because I sure as hell don't see a bunch of fucking people here!"

Eddie looked over at Gideon and leaned back against the wall, kicking his foot up and blowing smoke rings. "Well, there is that, I guess."

They stood under the awning and watched as the six flashlights moved farther and farther away from them and debated whether it would really be good news if one of the lights suddenly stopped moving. After twenty minutes, the lights had barely shown dim in the distance.

Eddie pushed swiftly off the wall. "This seriously fucking blows, Gideon! What kind of sick asshole calls in something like this for fun, huh?"

Gideon was crouched down and leaning back against the wall, his head hung. "I'm not sure that either of us really wants to know the answer to that question, my friend."

"Oh yeah . . . why would that be?"

"Because the question you should be asking is how did he know?"

"Know what?"

"Who outside of the VCU knew about the eyes, Eddie? We never released that in either death."

It hit Eddie in the face like a brick. "Aww shit . . . It was *him*!"

"Aww shit is right," Gideon said softly, "and now he's just fucking with us."

"Yeah but fucking with us, *why*? He's gotten away with it so far. Why screw with the police now?"

"I'm still working on that," Gideon replied, chewing on his nails as he stood up and walked a short distance away from the building. The rain was finally easing off, and he looked up, closing his eyes and allowing the cool mist to wash over his face.

"Gideon, you know us country folk don't take kindly to being fucked with . . . junior does not wanna make this personal."

Gideon's eyes still closed, he said, "Eddie . . . that's *exactly* what he wants to do."

With that, he opened his eyes and began a haggard pace slowly back down the hill toward the armory.

"Where are you going?" Eddie yelled.

"I'm going to crawl in a bottle for a few hours, think this through," he mumbled. "Call me if you find anything."

As he reached the car, the rain had stopped, and he popped the trunk release with the remote. Staring off into the darkness, he pulled off his coat and tossed it into the back. The day had been prophetic—and not in a good way. It was the first time in a long time that she had agreed to spend any time at all with him, and they get interrupted. Not once, but twice. He reached out and grabbed the trunk lid, the moonlight glinting off of something inside, catching his eye as the lid slammed shut. After another moment of somewhat confused reflection, he tapped the remote again as the lid slowly reopened. He peered down and spied it again, fainter this time, as he leaned into the trunk to brush it away. As he touched it, the coldness against his hand made him recoil a bit, and he lifted the coat closer to his face, staring at it. The silver button glistened brightly now in the bright light of the full moon. Confused for a moment, he argued with himself, swearing that he'd always thought his coat had black plastic buttons.

In another second, his confusion flashed over to disbelief as the familiarity of the object crystallized to clarity before him. His eyes closed, a sense of falling overwhelmed him as the images lunged toward him: the nickel-plated button lying on the edge of Stephanie's desk and the two coats on the rack. It had been Mattie who had come in late the morning after the murder. It had been he who hung his coat next to Gideon's. It had been Mattie sitting on the bench outside

Elizabeth's office that afternoon. The same bench that he would find Stephanie lying on hours later, and then there was the voice—

"Sounds good, Doc, mind if I hang out here till you wrap her up?"
"Absolutely," said the doc. "Gideon, I believe you know Mattie."
"Mattie cleans up after me," she said, "couldn't do this without him."
"Aww, Dr. Jernigan. Y-Y-You flatter me."

Suddenly, Gideon flashed back to the restaurant—the sounds of oblivious bar patrons chatting about banalities, as well as the monotonous din of dishes and glasses banging into plastic tubs as the waitstaff passed through the bar and into the kitchen.

"Oh fuck!" Gideon screamed. "He was there!"

He slammed the trunk back and jumped in, squealing the tires as he sped from the parking lot and out onto the Circle, barreling north toward Killearn. He flipped open the phone and punched in her number. After several rings and no answer, he pressed down harder on the pedal. The random thoughts kept racing through his mind, and he was getting more upset with himself by the mile for not seeing any of it earlier. All the pieces had fallen. Mattie *was* Abigail's son. She hadn't been sick the night before as Mattie had contended—she'd been *dead*! Very dead in fact, and Gideon's heart beat furiously as the moment of revelation assured him that Elizabeth was next if he didn't *hurry the fuck up*! Gideon was not about to let that happen. He'd let her down, somehow, before, but he had learned something from that. He'd told her not to worry, that everything would be all right. It would not happen again.

Gideon slid the car around the narrow corner onto her street and skidded to an abrupt stop in front of the house. Her car sat in the driveway, and he ran his hand across the hood, still warm. He walked slowly up the walk as a dim amber light trickled through the glass in the front door, emanating from the living room at the rear of the house. The hallway was off-center from the door, and he had no view. He knocked several times without an answer, harder each time, as he heard music coming from within that was louder than normal. A brief sense of relief arose as it occurred to him that perhaps she was just soaking in a warm tub as she was often prone to do. Gideon called her name through the door, still unanswered, and walked back off the porch and around the west side, a series of muffled yips catching his attention from around back. He eased through the pitch-black and peered over as he reached the privacy fence. On the other side, he spied the two Westies running up and down the stairs of the elevated deck. In theory, both dogs had been white, and he saw that they were both a dingy brown and covered in mud. His earlier relief gave way, again, as he knew that she would never leave either of the dogs outside in the rain like this. He grabbed the top of the fence and jumped over, landing awkwardly and falling against one of the wooden deck supports. Max was the first to reach him, licking the mud off of Gideon's face.

"Good to see you too, old friend."

Gideon grabbed the support and pulled himself up his eyes just above the level of the deck. Oscar was standing on his hind legs scratching furiously at the French doors, whimpering.

"What's the matter, Oscar? Where's mommy at?" he whispered. Oscar looked back at him briefly and returned his attention to the doors. The hair stood on his neck, and he removed his Glock from the holster on his belt. Oscar never would have ignored him like that, he thought. That dog had always been batshit crazy, and forever had the motor running. Something was not right.

He crept up the stairs, the thumping of the bass inside growing louder, almost familiar, as he approached the doors. As he peered in, he saw her. Elizabeth was seated at the dining room table, her back to him. He watched for a moment as she didn't move. A quick rap on the glass didn't change that. He felt for the handle and turned it slightly. The door gave way as the chill overtook him, and the familiar haunting riff from the sedan blared from the stereo in the corner. A light shone from the bedroom to his right, but there's no movement. He snapped his eyes back toward Elizabeth and moved around the couch slowly, closer to her from behind.

"Elizabeth?" he shouted over the music as he put his hand on her shoulder. His eyes grew wide as her head slumped down to her side. Gideon looked down: her hands were bound to the arms of the chair, and her eyes were closed. Gideon screamed her name again, laying the gun on the table next to her and felt for a pulse. In a moment—the music stopped.

He hadn't seen the approach. He had only felt the searing pain and the metallic peal resonating through his skull as he crumpled to the floor at the foot of her chair. He reached back instinctively, and his fingers grew warm as the blood wept over his hand. The light faded. When he awoke, still far from clarity, he rolled to his side and looked up as the now familiar face stood over him a few feet away, one of Elizabeth's titanium drivers in his hand.

Mathias smiled. "I must admit . . . I never cared much for the game, really," he said, speaking softly and deliberately. "But I do now see the appeal."

Gideon squeezed his eyes open and shut a few times, trying to make the multiple images come together. Slowly, he pulled his arm from under him until he came to rest on his elbow, still holding the back of his head as he looked dazedly up at him. Ordinarily, he would have had a comeback; this was not one of those times.

"I am truly sorry about that, Detective. I realize that my actions were quite rude and barbaric, and I must apologize . . . I mean a *club* for goodness' sake! How simply uncivilized. Anyway, I'm afraid it was quite necessary as I have an absolutely unabashed fear of guns, and well . . . you have a gun," he squeaked, smiling. "Or *had* a gun, rather. In any event, we felt that this was the best way to avoid any kind of undesirable confrontation between us . . . don't you agree?"

Gideon shook off the haze. "Who's *we*, Mathias?" His teeth clenched.

Mathias took a few steps back, laying the golf club on the table and running his fingers softly over the gun.

"And Heman the Ezrahite said unto God . . ." Mathias's was voice booming. "'You have taken from me my closest friends and have made me repulsive to them' . . . 'You have taken my companions and loved ones from me. The darkness is my closest friend'!"

"*Psalms?*" Gideon laughed, then winced as the pain in his head rudely reminded him of its presence. "You're quoting me Psalms, you asshole! That the best you *got?*"

A smile of recognition formed on Mathias's face. "Ahh, Detective, I see you are familiar with the good book, then?"

"I'm Catholic . . . technically," Gideon labored to speak. "I was an altar boy when I was a kid. So if anybody here has a right to be pissed off with the man upstairs, I'd say that alone makes me the winner, hands down! What? Do you think God's on your side with this shit! That you have some holy alliance with him? That he's put his stamp of approval on your sick bullshit?"

"God?" Mathias flashed a brief smile and laughed quietly. "Hardly, Detective. He has not been on my side for quite some time."

Mathias turned his back and walked over to the nearby bookshelf, peering over the titles. "Your girlfriend has simply had a dreadful taste in literature. Look at all these mysteries and thrillers on the shelves. Doesn't anyone understand that those who can *do* . . . and those who *can't*, resort to writing trashy novels in their spare time as a means of banishing the unbearable angst from their own lonely and pathetic lives?"

Mathias flipped his hands in the air and scoffed, "Why don't they just try yoga or something?"

Gideon tried to pull himself toward Elizabeth and cringed as the pain shot through his neck. "What did you do to her, Mathias?"

"Oh, don't worry just yet, Detective." Mathias turned briefly back to him with a quizzical look. "Actually, would you mind if I call you, Gideon? I feel like I've come to know you quite well over the last week. Anyway, your lovely Ms. Pierce here is quite alive for the moment." He spun around and took a few steps toward Gideon. "She's merely resting now, thanks to some *assistance* as it were. You see, she needed her rest. She has a big night ahead of her. Just a bit of something I mixed up to help her sleep. She can still hear us, I imagine. She must be absolutely petrified."

"If you touch one hair . . ."

"You'll what?" Mathias scoffed. "Oh, Gideon . . . how B movie of you. That was truly pathetic." Mathias moved closer to the table, brushing his hand across Elizabeth's face and looking nostalgic. "Say something powerful . . manly even, but please do not resort to burlesque clichés. It is simply beneath you. Your beloved is to be the final act in my play, the final piece of the puzzle that allows Mother to return to me once again. The eyes truly are the windows to the soul, Gideon. Did you not see that the first time you cast your gaze in her direction . . . and she in yours?"

The ringing in Gideon's head began to ebb somewhat, and he slid his left leg farther under Elizabeth's chair so that Mathias couldn't see, slowly running his hand down to his ankle and pulling the pant leg up, slightly exposing a bit of the second holster.

"What the hell are you talking about, you crazy fuck?" The pain in Gideon's head gave way to his blood pressure. "Do you honestly think that killing these women will bring Abigail back? You really are insane!"

"Well, there certainly is that, Detective Kane, but what I fail to grasp is that how a detective, a gatherer of facts, would have such a closed mind when it comes to matters with which he is merely unfamiliar? There are many things going on around you that you do not see, Detective Kane. Does that mean that they do not exist? Certainly not."

"Your mother is *dead,* asshole! It was an accident . . . let it go, and Elizabeth had nothing to do with any of it!" Gideon's rage welled as he looked up and saw her fingers moving. "If you touch her, Mathias . . . I assure you that I will reunite you with your mother tonight!"

Mathias's face suddenly contorted in anger as he grabbed her hair and pulled her head back, exposing her neck.

"You . . . detective . . . have no idea what has been taken from me! No idea what you would go through to get it back!

Mathias reached his other hand into his coat pocket and removed a number twenty-four scalpel, holding it up to the lamp over the table, the light glistening off the blade. Mathias sighed as he brought the blade back down, resting the flat end on her neck. Slowly, Mathias drew the blade lightly across her throat, the crimson beading along the line.

"You know, Gideon, I can understand why you pine for her . . . she's quite exquisite, magnificent features," he said as he lifted her eyelid, "and the most beautiful eyes this one. As green as a meadow I should say."

"Why, Mathias . . . why all of it? When did it start?"

"It started, my dear friend . . . when they took her from me. They all knew that she had done nothing wrong, that the company had caused the accident. Mr. Diaz had seen to that most efficiently as I recall. So I waited. Oh, I perfected my craft mind you, don't get me wrong . . . but I waited all those years for Diaz to covet something . . . to cherish something as much as that which was taken from *me*! And when the time was right, I watched . . . I waited . . . and then I took from him as he had done so many years before! Lex talionis! An eye for an eye, Gideon . . . no pun intended of course."

Gideon leaned forward, quietly unsnapping the holster. The Taurus CIA model five-shot .38 caliber revolver was his last resort—a sort of get-off-me gun. It wasn't nearly as powerful as his Glock, but at this range, it would do just fine.

"Why Stephanie, Mathias? Why her . . . where did she fit into this?"

Mathias ran his finger along the crimson line, bringing it up to his lips. "Ahh, the lovely Ms. Stephanie. Well, I simply could not allow you to stray from that which meant so much to you . . . to destroy what has taken so long for the two of you to grow. I've seen the way you look at this one, Gideon . . . this angel that sits here before us."

Gideon's head throbbed as he dropped his gaze to the floor. "What the hell are you talking about, Mathias?"

Mathias shook his head, frustrated. "Dear, Gideon . . . it is love. How do you not see?"

"See what, *Mathias*? That you've been stalking me for the past three days?"

"I watch, Mr. Kane . . . that is my gift. I see all that those around me cannot see. I do not take a life simply to do so, dear boy, on the contrary." Mathias leaned over and kissed her eye softly. "There must be true love in these eyes in order for the soul to travel there. It must be at the point when her soul finally realizes what it has lost . . . what is most important . . . what it has forsaken. That is why you were brought here this night. So that she may see that which she has denied all this time. To finally see . . . through *her* eyes . . . a love most genuine. That is what is required for my task."

At this point, Gideon lay almost beneath her, and he had no shot at Mathias's head or body without shooting through Elizabeth. Through the legs of the chair, however, he saw Mathias's ankle, looking as big as a Christmas ham.

"It almost seems a shame, Detective, to waste such beauty, but they shall look wonderful in my collection."

Mathias brought the blade down toward her eye just as consciousness returned to her. Her screams could hardly drown out the report as Mathias crumbled.

"Gideon, please!" she screamed. Gideon looked away from Mathias briefly to see the tears as she looked down at him and pleaded, whispering, "Help me, Gideon." Elizabeth's screams turned to sobbing as she looked down at him. Her eyes—he'd never seen her eyes as beautiful before.

The pain tore through his leg, the scalpel flying as he released it, his hands reaching down to cover the blood and shattered bone that was his ankle, and he fell to the floor on the side of her chair opposite Gideon. Mathias was now at his level, and Gideon tried to muddle through the voices screaming in his head to blow his goddamn brains out. Gideon looked over near the leg of the chair—the scalpel lay on the floor between them—as Mathias began to crawl toward it.

"Kill him!" Elizabeth screamed as she struggled to free her hands from the chair.

Gideon stared down the barrel, the sight resting over the scalpel as Mathias's hand came into view. The trigger felt heavier than it ever had as Gideon pulled back with his remaining strength. In that instant, all sound vanished, peaceful silence as he could almost see the bullet leave the barrel in slow motion, rising slightly as he watched it hit. The ashen pallor of Mathias's hand effused in the deep red color of unimaginable pain. He recoiled to his back, grabbing the shattered bone and clutching it tightly.

Mathias began to laugh as he screamed, "C'mon, Kane! Do you think this is *over*? We are joined forever, you and I!"

He continued to cackle hysterically as Gideon looked back up at Elizabeth. "You okay?" he begged as she nodded in the affirmative.

"Good." His head fell down to his other arm as he laughed. "Told ya I was gonna take care of you."

"You always do . . . don't you?" she whispered, returning the smile.

32

The red and blue lights flickered off the front of the house as Gideon sat in the doorway of the ambulance next to Elizabeth. The paramedics said she'd been given some kind of depressant that was making her go in and out of consciousness. She wasn't awake long enough for them to determine what Mathias had given her, so they'd made the decision that she was going to the hospital for at least one day of rest. One of the EMTs was busy cleaning out the gash on the back of his head as he stared out across the road and pulled the heavy wool blanket around him as the other paramedics wheeled Mathias toward the other truck.

"Ya know something, Gideon," Eddie said as he took a slow drag from the Winston, "the next time you leave to go save the world from the crazy fuckers . . . how 'bout yelling across the parking lot for some help first?"

Gideon took a breath and turned around watching Liz lying on the gurney.

"She's gonna be just fine, Gideon," Eddie said. "No injuries other than whatever sort of fucked up cocktail he gave to her. She's just gonna need to sleep it off whatever it is."

Gideon stood up and sighed. "Eddie . . . I don't think she can sleep that long . . . What about him?"

"Who, crazy boy? Oh, he's fucked. You gave him a nice little limp to go along with that stutter of his. Unfortunately, he's gonna live though . . . he's a real chick magnet now. Listen, Gideon, I'm not

SEE NO EVIL (THE GIDEON KANE FILES)

second-guessing you now so don't take it that way but . . . why didn't you kill him?"

In the last twenty minutes, Gideon had asked himself that question a thousand times.

A search of Mathias's house eventually turned up enough evidence to give him the electric chair. Crime scene techs filed in and out of the wooden shed like ants in a colony, carrying boxes of unassuming glass jars as others tilled through the upper layers of soil in the backyard. Ryden stood outside the shed looking down at the ground, shaking his head and realizing how close he'd come to either knowing the whole truth or winding up in one of the boxes. Gideon knew that a trial for Mathias would be at least a year or two away, and he was pretty sure that the state of Florida, in its infinite wisdom, would eventually determine that Mathias Arbin was too crazy to kill. A quiet and tranquil eight by five concrete cell in the maximum security wing of the Chattahoochee State mental health facility would have to suffice for the time being.

The man walked unassumingly and deliberately into the front lobby of the Chattahoochee facility, placing his black leather briefcase on the floor as he stepped up to the front desk. The man was in his forties, dark-skinned, with salt-and-pepper hair in a neatly pressed three-button black pinstriped suit.

"Gabriel Asher to see Mathias Arbin," he stated to the guard across the desk.

Without looking up, the guard responded, "Nobody sees Arbin without being on the list."

"Oh, but, sir," Asher's voice deepened, "I *am* on the list."

The guard momentarily looked up from his magazine and stared into the eyes of Gabriel Asher. His first thought was that they seemed black and empty, bottomless even, and he was transfixed. There were no other independent thoughts that followed.

"Have a seat for a moment, and I will buzz you in," the guard droned as if talking in his sleep.

"Thank you, my good man," Asher replied as he bent over, retrieved the briefcase, and strode over to the heavy metal door to his right. Asher grabbed the handle as the buzzer sounded and the door clicked open.

Mathias lay on his bunk as he stared up at the fluorescent lights, the ballasts humming with annoying frequency. He rolled his head back toward the cinderblock wall on his right, his thumbnail scraping another line in the dingy, depressing, mint green paint completing the message: *I see you, Gideon Kane.*

ABOUT THE AUTHOR

Scott DelBeato is a sixteen-year veteran of Florida law enforcement and is a US Navy submarine force veteran and graduate of Florida State University. As a finance and math major in college, Scott spent a fateful Friday night on a ride along with a close friend who was a Tallahassee police department patrol officer. That night, filled with adrenaline and purpose, led to a life-altering career change. What followed was a law enforcement career that would ultimately lead to the investigation and capture of serial killer Gary Michael Hilton. Sergeant DelBeato has worked as a patrol officer, property and persons detective, and SWAT officer. The *Gideon Kane Files* are a type of catharsis for the author in an attempt to unsee some of the worst of people and the best of people at their worst.

CPSIA information can be obtained
at www.ICGtesting.com
Printed in the USA
LVOW10s0308171116

513337LV00001B/81/P